Dr. Elko gave me a phrase I used in the 2015 NFC Championship Game: "Live the Moment." I taught that to the team. They did.

Ron Rivera, Head Coach, Carolina Panthers

Dr. Kevin Elko shares a unique lens to view through and a powerful message to grow into. He has a servant's heart that will make you better personally and professionally.

Clint Hurdle, Manager, Pittsburgh Pirates

I have been fortunate to know Dr. Elko, both personally and professionally for over 20 years. I have watched his teaching, insights and creative ideas play a huge role in not only my career, but that of many others in the world of highly competitive sports. He is a tremendous mentor and a great resource for advice. His concepts on training the mind and motivating individuals, are always in the forefront and on the cutting edge!

Butch Davis, Head Football Coach University of Miami, ESPN Game Day Analyst

Dr. Elko is the best guest in the history of our show. His conversations with us are always compelling and important. His messages to the audience are always heartfelt and filled with compassion. You'll love this book.

Paul Finebaum, Host, *The Finebaum Show*, SEC Network, ESPN

Dr. Elko has been a blessing in my life. I am a better leader and connector because of his guidance. His way of looking at leadership and core values hits home to coaches, men, fathers, and athletes. He is caring and direct and cuts to the point with his own incredible stories and genuine realism. Success as a leader is about connection and Dr. Elko knows exactly how to connect and deliver his message!

Dave Doren, Head Football Coach, North Carolina State University

The message in this book is a game changer that helps people meet their potential. It will transform your life so you can impact others in so many ways. This message has been a part of the culture of our championship teams.

Sarah Patterson, Legendary University of Alabama
Gymnastic Coach

Dr. Elko's message on the power of grit had a lot to do with our championship at Florida State—we teach it over and over. The message in this book will take you higher, it did the Noles.

Jimbo Fisher, Head Football Coach,
Florida State University

Dr. Elko's message, which is in *The Sender*, focused our team and was a big part of our run to the College World Series. And it will help elevate your organization to new heights.

Dan McDonnell, Head Baseball Coach,
The University of Louisville

I've known Dr. Elko for almost twenty years. His presence, delivery method, and words are timeless. No matter the audience, he always makes a connection with the audience that makes you feel that he is speaking directly to you. I've personally witnessed him talking to groups ranging from financial advisors to national championship football teams and results are always the same. Everyone leaves his talks with a better understanding of themselves and how life's obstacles are what you make them. He helped me personally in my own fight with cancer and I know that he will help you too.

Tom Moffit, Head Football Strength Coach,
Louisiana State University

This exact message and these letters sent to Coach Pagano are what I listened to as soon as I got my [cancer] diagnosis and started on my journey,

Chris Mortensen, ESPN NFL Analyst

Dr. Elko is the best I've seen in helping young men focus on "keeping the main thing the main thing"! He has given us the tools to help manage daily conflicts and stress while helping our team "lock in" and remove outside distractions. He helps better prepare our student athletes both on and off the field.

Scott Cochran, Head Football Strength Coach,
The University of Alabama

I've known Dr. Elko for a decade. It wasn't until I found myself using his phrases in my everyday life that I realized the profound impact he has had on my life. Through his powerful words and teachings he shows us how to embrace times of challenge with courage, hope, and a little humor.

Greg P. Cicotte, Head of U.S. Wealth Management
and Distribution,
Jackson National Life Insurance Company

Copyright © 2016 by Kevin Elko and Bill Beausay

Published by Worthy Inspired, an imprint of Worthy Publishing Group, a division of Worthy Media, Inc., One Franklin Park, 6100 Tower Circle, Suite 210, Franklin, TN 37067.

WORTHY is a registered trademark of Worthy Media, Inc.

HELPING PEOPLE EXPERIENCE THE HEART OF GOD

Library of Congress Cataloging-in-Publication Data

Names: Elko, Kevin, 1958- author. | Beausay, William, 1957- author.
Title: The sender : when the right words make all the difference / Kevin Elko and Bill Beausay.
Description: Franklin, TN : Worthy Inspired, 2016.
Identifiers: LCCN 2016001191 | ISBN 9781617957321 (hardcover)
Subjects: LCSH: Cancer--Patients--Fiction. | Life change events--Fiction. | Football coaches--Fiction. | Letter writing--Fiction. | BISAC: FICTION / Christian / General. | GSAFD: Christian fiction. | Epistolary fiction.
Classification: LCC PS3605.L427 S46 2016 | DDC 813/.6--dc23
LC record available at http://lccn.loc.gov/2016001191

ISBN: 978-1-61795-732-1
ISBN: 978-1-61795-807-6 (special edition)

For foreign and subsidiary rights, contact rights@worthypublishing.com

Cover Design: David Carlson / Studio Gearbox

Printed in the United States of America

16 17 18 19 20 21 LBM 10 9 8 7 6 5 4 3 2 1

the
sender

*a story about when right words
make all the difference*

Kevin Elko and Bill Beausay

WORTHY.
Inspired

Introduction

SEVERAL GAMES INTO THE 2012 pro football season, Indianapolis Colts Head Coach Chuck Pagano was diagnosed with acute promyelocytic leukemia. It was a devastating revelation that brought major outpouring of attention and care from both inside and outside the NFL. Chuck immediately relinquished his role as head coach and entered into an onerous 90-day chemo protocol. His team, inspired by the plight of their severely ill leader rallied and nearly made it to the Superbowl.

In the spring of 2014 I was having a casual conversation with renowned sports performance consultant Kevin Elko Ph.D. who shared an amazing footnote to the story. Kevin consults with many pro and college level football teams. He was a very close friend of Pagano's. Every day for the entire 90-day chemotherapy treatment cycle he'd sent his friend Chuck an audio-letter of encouragement, stories, anecdotes and motivation. *Every day*. Kevin shared these letters with me, all 90 of them. I read the transcripts and was thunderstruck by what was there. I immediately thought that everyone in any position of life, good or bad should be so lucky to have a friend like Kevin sending them letters like these. They were just that good. Simple, funny, homespun and touching in every way. Probably Kevin's best work ever.

Fiction allows you great latitude in storytelling. So, starting with little more than a pile of letters we created this fictional tale. It's an account of a football coach struck down with cancer. Coach Charlie Cristo is "every man" fighting in the trenches of life, then is completely blindsided by a dreaded illness. But through a series of anonymous, daily letters our coach Charlie learns some profound life lessons, faith lessons, and faces tests on each of them. Some tests he passes and others not so much. But he practices and grows and changes.

The letters that appear in this book are the actual letters Elko sent to Pagano.

Our hope is that this story touches you and causes you to consider some of your own personal challenges and lessons. *Our ho*pe is that you take these lessons and use them in your own journey. *Our hope* is that you find a way to serve others with what you learn here. *Our hope* is that you'll fight and sweat and grind and love no matter what happens to you. And *our hope* is that you'll write someone that you love a letter of encouragement, triumph and peace because you've been changed by what happened to you here.

CHAPTER .01

THERE'S NO SELF-PITY with cancer . . .

Charlie winced, rolled over and looked out the window. It was gray and gloomy.

Or is it "There's no self-pity in football"? he wondered, trying to get his mind off the pain. He'd read that somewhere and couldn't remember. He squinted into the fog outside his window, trying to recall. His head was just as hazy as it was outside—the drugs did that to him. His arm ached from the needles. The docs had suggested installing a port-a-cath, but he'd resisted. It sounded terminal to him. It was time for it, though. His throat was raw. The hospital bedsheets caught, then tugged and twisted his bad leg. His body twitched back hard.

"God, that hurt!" He cursed, gritting and wincing again.

Everything hurt during chemo: bone pain, nausea, and that constant headache. This was way worse than he had feared. His spirit grew dark. The only thing he felt like doing was crying. But that was not allowed. Then, the unthinkable words drifted through his brain fog—"God, please let me die." Ache upon ache.

The cancer had been diagnosed just two months back but Charlie's outlook on life was already pretty bleak. He'd been unhappy, discontented, for a long time. He'd lost touch with joy, was wrapped up in worry. *Gotta make more money. Who will pay the bills? Pay for college for the girls? Will I be there to dance at their weddings? Everybody seems to be going about their lives at full speed. What about me?* He'd been plagued by thoughts like this for some time. The cancer just inflamed all his old anxieties.

But now his body was dwindling too. He could see that in the mirror.

From time to time, his patience would snap and he'd explode at somebody. Anybody would do, as long as he got it out. He had to get his mind off this killing pain and fatigue; his screwed-up balance; meat-red sore throat; fever; the dryness, metal taste and ulcers in his mouth; baldness . . . and the constant allover ache. And this was only phase one of three. Daily body massages eased the throbbing, but the relief only lasted so long. The nurses kept a close watch on his meds, but most of the time he just wanted another hit.

The cancer support group wasn't helping much. "You'll get better!" they'd say, pouring forth heaping ladles of chicken-soup encouragement.

Oh my God, please . . . wipe those smiles off your faces, he'd think, his voice echoing angrily inside his head. *Just shut up; you have no clue. You lie here for a month and then see if you're so chirpy.* Their sunny bull crap was more than he could take most days.

Charlie talked to himself a lot.

His mind drifted again. He felt empty, angry, pained, driven, hopeless. Emotional and spiritual agony blackened every moment. He was limp from exhaustion. Vince Lombardi's words drifted into his thoughts, something Lombardi was quoted as saying shortly before he succumbed to cancer: *Fatigue makes cowards of us all.*

Charlie chafed, grimaced, and clenched his teeth in defiance, but he'd spent all the energy he could muster. He was just too tired to fight. Maybe he was a coward. Or maybe he was just tired of being tired and beaten up over and over again.

And then, just when his mind-set couldn't get worse, it did.

His thoughts hopscotched around with little purpose or control. He drifted more deeply into his positively messed-up situation: his aimless and frustrating career, money problems, his new job now hanging by a thread, a wife who'd emotionally checked out, and now cancer. *Cancer.* The word evoked so much. He could see it clearly within him: dark and ghoulish; gray-black sludge in his bones, caustic yellow-jelly pus leaching into his aching joints, dark bruises on his skin, bones sticking out all over, the feeling of being eaten alive from the inside by a dark, smelly, fiery demon.

He was angry, resentful, and hated everything. And it was all compounded by unyielding exhaustion.

His psyche raced round and round in silent desperation. Then that fat, obnoxious nursing assistant came in. The one with bad breath and the tattoos that made her look cheap. She was good with those needles though. No pain. He never gave her enough credit for that. How could she have wrecked herself with all that ink? *Disgusting*, he thought.

Snapping at the nursing staff was his trademark. His reputation as a difficult and angry patient had ballooned recently. The truth was he'd been snapping at people for years. He couldn't remember when it started. All he knew was that his uncontrolled anger and attitude issues had gotten him canned—or simply not renewed—at coaching job after coaching job. It cost him a lot of friendships too.

Through his own actions he'd become an empty, cussing, hurting mess. It was an appalling dilemma with no way out. He wanted to just collapse and cry, but he had already collapsed and the tears would not come. There was no bottom left. But there's no self-pity in cancer.

His vision, attitude, and demeanor were completely septic; his hope was gone. The disease owned Charlie.

HE MUST'VE DOZED OFF during the pity party he wasn't sup-posed to have. He awoke in a surprisingly pleasant post-nap mood. That was rare. What wasn't rare was how low he could crash when Bing walked in.

Bing Macklemore was a round man with a fat face as red as a cherry. He was receiving therapy in a room down the hall. He had considerably more energy than Charlie and seemed to constantly seek attention. He was loud, obnox-ious, and chatty. He chafed on Charlie. He was a profes-sional gambler, winning a fortune playing poker online and telling anyone who would listen just how great he was. He gabbed constantly.

Always good for a few lies, Charlie thought as he watched that swollen, crimson moon face come toward him.

Bing was about Charlie's age and used to play high school football, which he told anyone who would listen.

Charlie could take him for a few minutes, but that was about it.

"These letters are pretty good, Coach," Bing said, holding up several folded pieces of paper in his hand and moving toward Charlie's bedside. Without being invited he took a seat.

"What letters?" Charlie asked.

Bing waved the papers and partially exposed one to give Charlie a peek.

"Oh, those," Charlie said, vaguely recalling giving Bing the letters to make him get lost.

Charlie had been receiving them from the day he'd entered the hospital, but had only read the first one. Come to think of it now, that first one he read talked about self-pity. That's where that strange repetitive thought was coming from. *Hm.*

The letters came almost every day. The nurses would throw them into an old shoebox. The box was filling with unopened envelopes. He assumed they were fan mail or "Let's all feel sorry for poor ol' Charlie" notes, so he'd handed a few to Bing, one to this nurse or that nurse.

"Why does this guy keep calling you Dog?" Bing asked.

"Dog? Excuse me?" Charlie sat up an inch, anger flaring in his eyes.

"Yeah, *DOG*!" Bing grinned, knowing a nerve when he'd hit one.

Charlie ignited. "What the—gimme that!"

Summoning all his energy, he lurched upward out of bed and snatched the letters from Bing's puffed-up hand. One tore before Bing let go.

He glanced over it quickly. At the bottom of the page was written in big letters, "Size 9 ring when you win the championship, Dog."

WHAAA? Who was this? "I'm fighting for my life and this person wants a ring when I win the championship?"

Equal parts seething and curious, Charlie immersed himself in the letter. Bing, seeing that he'd lost Charlie's attention, rose and waddled toward the door.

"Let me know what you think, Dog," he said over his shoulder.

Charlie never noticed him leave.

He held the letter for a moment, then dropped it at his side as his thoughts took off at a gallop. *Getting to the big leagues of coaching is a waiting game*, he thought for no particular reason. The equation is well known: being the right person with the right pedigree, the right connection, the right opportunity—and some luck. Charlie had opportunity after opportunity to go big-time, only to fumble on the one-yard line because he was not "the right person." He had been told that so many times. He knew it. He was sick of it. He had no idea what it meant or how to fix it.

After years of fumbling himself down the coaching ladder, he'd landed a coaching job at Seminole Valley High School. Head coach of the one-time powerhouse Alabama football machine was good, but small-time. It wasn't his dream job, but dream jobs are difficult to make real when all you seem to be able to do is make enemies. The fans were delirious with excitement, though, that such a "big star" would be there to coach their team.

Yeah, Charlie was a glory-days hero in Crimson Tide country. He was a quarterback phenom beloved by everyone. But fan love is fickle. Who you used to be doesn't really matter. Fail to live up to today's expectations and, like the Romans, they'll have your head on a platter.

The initial excitement of Charlie Cristo running the team turned sour following the Bucks' lethargic 1–2 start. The fans, administration, student body, and the press were looking for a platter. It seemed like it happened in a blink.

And now the cancer. His spirit slipped into blackness as he contemplated the reality of his situation.

In a moment of clarity, he realized his problems had started way before Seminole Valley High. He pressed his pounding head back into the pillow. He wanted another hit of morphine, but the nurses insisted not for another hour.

His memory drifted back to that really bad, sun-drenched afternoon in Tuscaloosa. The University of Tennessee Volunteers were in town and the Tide was rolling toward another national championship. It would be a clash of giants. Just get past the Vols. The Big Orange was always tough and Coach Bear Bryant warned his team about misjudging them. But they had Charlie, the star quarterback, the man many Alabamans considered a gridiron god. Confidence was running high.

At the beginning of the fourth quarter the Crimson

Tide had the game and their national championship hopes solidly handled. Then . . .

Charlie dropped back to throw a routine screen pass when he saw a streak of orange coming from his left. Somebody missed a block. The hit was hard. Then a thunderous *CRACK!* and pain unlike anything he'd ever felt.

All the players on the field heard the nauseating snap and tear. The crowd went silent. No sounds; just muffled anguish. Charlie lay writhing on the ground. He rolled around out there on the field of Bryant-Denny stadium for a long time. The god humbled at the center of the sprawling script *A*.

Charlie sighed, and was back in his hospital bed. There was horrible pain in his joints. Cancer really hurts. But he wouldn't trade it for the pain he felt that terrible afternoon many years ago.

In a few moments the deep bone ache and muscle ache subsided a bit and his thoughts drifted backward in time again. He recalled that at the instant of the hit he knew it was serious. He panicked. He was a young man then, but for the first time in his life he was flat on his back and not getting up. He suddenly felt very human and very, very afraid.

But football doesn't care. Football doesn't cry. The dream was over. Charlie was done and fate had different plans. His dream ship had marooned him, broken and alone. It was a whole new game now, the beginning of a very long and difficult story. No self-pity allowed.

He snapped back into the present moment as he tried to clear his burned-out throat. The pain was enormous. *What happened? What was this cancer all about anyway? Why me?*

THE SURGEONS DID THE BEST they could to fix Charlie but he had a permanent limp from the hit. He was twenty-two years old, and his dream of playing in the pros was over. He'd be lucky to walk normally again. Outside of pro ball, he never had any other vision for himself. Football was just the perfect place for him and there was never any need to think further. Now the future was . . . blank. Nothing. No vision. No light. No hope. Maybe he'd drive a city bus or be a gym teacher.

Ugh.

In the years following college graduation he'd slowly begun the process of building a life and a future completely from scratch. It was the toughest fight he'd ever faced. Few people know what it's like to have your whole future, your entire vision and identity, stripped from you in one appalling second.

But here he was with his loser's limp, hobbling through life, trying to get something going.

The Midas touch of his playing days had vanished. It was replaced with a roiling and frustrating pain that radiated off him like heat. He bumped from one college assistant-coaching job to another. How many times had he heard that he just wasn't the "right fit"? Twenty years' worth. Never breaking through into the big time. His attitude grew more corrosive with time. He became known as difficult and unlikable, missing opportunity after opportunity to rise in the coaching ranks.

His friends and mentors were as encouraging as they could be, but the life of an assistant college football coach is a grind. Lonely nights on the road recruiting. Relentless hours during the season. Film, film, and more film. There was little recognition and less money. His wife, Eve, was done with it long ago. Charlie believed she held on in hope that the next season would bring a more secure job, better benefits, and maybe even the big break. But if he was honest with himself, Charlie knew that Eve's hope had faded long ago and she was mentally and emotionally done.

Then the call came from Seminole Valley. Coaching his high school alma mater. They had a winning tradition back in Charlie's day, but that was long ago. Still, he would have accolades, prestige, and nights at home. It was an imperfect solution to the perfect mess, but you take what you can get.

Eve was inconsolable about this move down. She'd secretly dreamed of Charlie finally going up to the pros. She saw herself sitting on the plush thrones of the owner's suite, dressed to kill, watching her superman coaching Super Bowls. She envisioned herself waving from the towering heights of her cushy loge, beckoning to her conquering hero, then draping her adoring arms around him amid flying confetti.

Her disappointment about him going back to coach high school ball turned into naked bitterness and outright anger. She had suffered so much for so many years for this? She resolved to resist this downward move as long as possible. Though she still lived in their home and took great care of the girls, she was over it—over *him*.

Charlie was crushed and angry as ever. Finally a chance at some redemption and the person he most wanted to share it with was a shell. *No self-pity in marriage* leapt to his mind as he recounted his plight. Eve was helping out during his treatment, but things between them were always tense and unsettled.

Due to the many complications likely in Charlie's cancer-therapy protocol, every round was done as an inpatient. Normally chemo is done on an outpatient basis, but the pain, exhaustion, blood-monitoring complications, and extreme nausea that accompanied the aggressive intervention Charlie was receiving were unmanageable in outpatient care. Charlie was told the first round of the three-phase treatment would be difficult; the second round was usually much worse. They hoped they would be able to get to the third.

The head nurse during his extended hospital stays was a happy woman Charlie would begin seeing as an angel: Lisa. She seemed to always carry an aura of big joy. It never really registered with Charlie until he became more accustomed to the routine, but her effervescence meant a lot to him. When she was around he just felt better.

Lisa entered the room, interrupting Charlie's constant

"failure-at-everything" mental beating. In her hand was a letter.

"Another one, Coach" she said, waving it gently.

Charlie glanced down at the "Dog" letter Bing had brought earlier. Something about the memory of giving Bing that letter alerted his mind. Charlie had a sudden recognition, an almost out-of-body observation that this cancer was making him act crazy. He was high, low, sharp, dull, depressed, sleepy—all in five minutes. He couldn't control it. And the letters . . . they were the strangest things. He'd never really considered them.

Lisa reached to pick up the "Dog" letter and toss it into the shoebox with the others, but Charlie stopped her.

"Are these still coming?" he asked. "I've been a little groggy."

"Almost every single day since you've been here, Coach," she said.

During his first month in the hospital his clarity of mind would come and go. During the alert times he became vaguely conscious of the constant rhythm of these strange letters. They were easy to recognize: they had no return address.

His mind cleared and the letter sparked his curiosity.

Lisa put the letter on the tray next to his bed. Charlie just stared at the envelope as Lisa checked his vitals and adjusted the equipment. She patted Charlie on the foot as she left and said, "Remember you're being pruned, honey. Get better, not bitter."

She was so nice to him. She surely didn't deserve the way he'd treated her.

Charlie smiled weakly, then it dawned on him what she'd said: "Get better, not bitter." He'd heard that before somewhere. It was blurry, but wait—it was the first letter, the only one he'd read. That first letter came out of nowhere. It was neatly typed, about a page long. Then they just kept coming and coming, and he lost interest. Handed them to nurses, to Bing, and to who knows who else.

Charlie reached down, picked up the shoebox, and slowly flipped through the mostly unopened letters. He found that very first one.

Hey Charlie, it's me—
John 15, in the Bible, is one of the last discussions Christ had with his disciples. He opened up the discussion by talking about pruning and husbandry and then he started talking about how you will be pruned: all the leaves and stems that don't bear fruit will be taken away and the ones that have fruit will be pruned to make them more fruitful.

Then Christ's half-brother, James—who was re-counting the story—said be "glad for your adversity." Be glad for your suffering. It will teach you patience, endurance, and long-suffering.

These merge into a simple idea: be better, not bitter. You are getting pruned. You are being tested for endurance. You should be doing back flips. Be happy for endurance. Be happy for long-suffering. You should throw a party. It teaches you patience.

Here we go, let me pull this all together: When I got with my wife, she loved to bike. She was in biking clubs. She would go on fifty-mile rides. Charlie, I'm not a biker. I always had a basketball or a football in my hands. Biking? It's a little too groovy for me.

But I wanted to be close to my wife. So I bought a bike and now I'm biking. I got into the things that she's into because I wanted to be close to her.

To get close to God, get into the things that He's into. He's into the poor, He's into the suffering, He's into the lonely, and He's into the sick. That's what God is into.

I had a friend that I played football with. He was a defensive back with me. His name was Chuck but we called him Woodchuck. I grew up back in

*the hollers and we all had nicknames for each other:
Snake, Beaver, Possum, Frog, Woodchuck—you know,
animals. Anyway, Woodchuck was wild. And he got
some kind of disease where a virus attacked the outer
sheath of his spinal cord. And he called me. He was in
a rehab in Morgantown, West Virginia. Crazy guy. I
walked in. There was nothing to him. They had to pick
him up just to move him. He was screaming when they
moved him.*

*Despite the screaming they put him in a wheel-
chair. Then he said to me, "Wheel me down to the
cafeteria." So I wheel him down to the cafeteria. As
we moved along he suddenly told me to stop. A woman
was coming the other way. She looked like she was
about eighty or ninety years old. He looked at her
and said, "Who da man?" She said, "You da man." I
could tell he trained her. He told me to go ahead. So I
walked again.*

*Even in the middle of whatever he's going through,
he took time out to be kind and through the awful
pruning, he got closer to God.*

Lessons get learned, then lessons get tested.

*You'll be tested. You are going to come out of
here and you are going to be more drawn to people
and more drawn to helping people and being kinder*

than you've ever been. That's your test. The tree will be pruned and where it's pruned, it will bear fruit. You were selected to be pruned. And you are going to be different than you ever were. Get better, not bitter.

—The Sender

PS: You da man!

It seemed to be assumed that Charlie would know who "the Sender" was. And he had some hunches—whoever it was seemed to have good knowledge about Charlie's life, history, challenges, and habits—but was too exhausted and weak to try to figure it out. The letter was a little religious. But that was OK too. The words had power and precision that surprised him, religion or no.

That first letter contained some diamonds worth remembering . . . and sharing. He wondered if all the letters in his little box were the same.

He'd been fortunate in the support shown for him through his ordeal, but was mostly too tired and bitter to notice. His team, coaches, and community had rallied: heads shaved in unity, raffles, fund-raising events, "Charlie Strong" T-shirts, and more. On his good days he could rally his attitude enough to feel a glint of gratitude. But it was work.

He quickly read a couple more letters. The letters always

seemed to have just the right message. They had an uncanny confidence . . . a *certainty* about them. They were godsends.

It crossed Charlie's mind that he might use some ideas from the letters for the pep talk he'd promised to give his team when he was released from the hospital. But at that moment doing a pep talk seemed impossible.

So tired. The spells of fatigue would sweep over him in seconds. Charlie put the letters down and fell quietly into a deep sleep.

CHAPTER .06

ABOUT AN HOUR LATER he woke and felt a little better. He reached for the letter Lisa had delivered earlier, anxious now to hear more good words. He glanced up at the clock on the wall.

"Dang it!" he croaked out loud. When he heard his own voice, it sounded hoarse. *Cancer hoarse.*

It was two o'clock. He'd missed his show.

He'd developed a guilty pleasure. He knew he should be working on that new package of plays to help his re-surging Bucks into the state playoffs, not watching *General Hospital* at one o'clock every day. But it was just so good; great fodder for chatting with the nurses when he felt better. It would be back on tomorrow, he reasoned. Not much will have changed anyway. Besides, this letter business made him feel a flicker of freshness somewhere within. Somehow, he just felt better.

He tore off the end of the newly delivered envelope, pulled out the paper, and quickly unfolded it.

Cancer is like a ball game. Here comes the cancer, chemo takes a shot and knocks it out. Cancer drops back, regroups, comes back stronger, and takes on the chemo. The chemo takes a shot back. Like a ball game.

But sooner or later in this volley, a message gets stated loud and clear. "I'm not giving up." One side sends a message: "I'm not giving up. I'm an all-day sucker." And when that message comes, the other one says, "I'm out." It's just like a ball game.

When Holyfield and Tyson boxed, Holyfield sent a message through his punches and his eyes and his energy. "I'm not going to quit." So Tyson said, "I'm biting his ear and getting out of here."

Go into this thing, Charlie, just send a message— send everything a message—send cancer this message with everything you are doing, "I ain't quittin'. I'm not stopping. You bring whatever you've got. I'm punching you back." And then sooner or later, like in a ball game, they get the message. He ain't quitting.

You go into this thing cold-blooded. "I'm here to get the job done. You bring whatever you've got to bring, but I'm not quitting. For my wife, I'm not quitting. For my daughters, I'm not quitting. You bring whatever you've got to bring, I really don't care."

For all those ballplayers who shaved their heads for you, "I'm not quitting. I've got stuff waiting on me. You bring whatever you've got to bring; we'll be here forever."

I met an old, old scout for Dallas who played for Bear Bryant in the way, way early days down at Texas. Maybe you know him; you played for the Bear. Anyway, he wanted to be captain and Bear Bryant came and tried to run him off. He made him run sprints all night long in the middle of the night. Finally after hours of this the kid went over to one of the assistants and said, "We can be here forever. You can run me until the sun comes up, goes back down, and comes up again. I'm not quitting." Bear Bryant stopped it and said, "He's my captain."

You tell all your assistant coaches of the cancer team that you are not quitting. You tell the Mike Tyson of the cancer team, "Bite my ear, I'm going to keep boxing." Protect your ears, Dog. Your hair's gone. That's a bad look. You just send a message to everybody—"I'm not going to quit. No ears, I'm not quittin'. The spirit will not surrender here."

—The Sender

PS: I'm an all-day sucker.

Charlie put the letter down grinning. Good stuff. He ran his hand over his bare head. He felt his ear. Yup; a chaw-eared bald guy *would* be a bad look. He laughed a little. Then suddenly he realized how dark he'd been on the inside, and how this little ray of encouragement peeked through . . . and felt good. Then he had the strangest thought: *Who else needs to hear this?* It felt strange to think of sharing with someone. He started thinking of people.

A name popped to mind. Johnny "Leatherhead" Picasso. Yeah, Picasso needed it. Picasso was an assistant coach at Seminole Valley who had taken up the challenge of head coach in Charlie's absence. He picked up the nickname because he was so old they joked that he must've worn a leather helmet back in the day. He was also the PE teacher and an artiste on gap blocking and pocket protection. He'd been a line coach at Seminole Valley for years and was much loved. He was even named on some of the old tarnished championship plaques sitting in the high school's trophy case. He was a loyal and competent assistant, great with the linemen, but rumor had it that he was upset at Charlie being hired. He wanted the job. But that wasn't gonna happen: coaches who played in leather helmets aren't considered cutting edge for up-tempo modern teams. Not at Seminole Valley anyway.

Picasso enjoyed his head-coaching job tremendously.

He was doing a great job too. Though Charlie worried for a second about helping his competition, his urge to pass the lesson on was stronger. Charlie loved his team and would do whatever was needed to make them winners. A lot rode on winning.

Coaching football players had taught Charlie a great deal about learning lessons. Especially life lessons. Those kinds of lessons are slippery. They have a way of dissolving into the noise of daily existence, and then disappearing altogether. We've all experienced this: hearing a story or a lesson we've already heard before and being astonished all over again. Something you already know, but forgot you knew. It isn't worth much if it's forgotten.

Charlie had learned a technique from another great coach to overcome this natural tendency. The habit was simple enough: put the lesson into play immediately. Share it, talk about it, do it, preach it, coach it, write it, spread it around out loud to another person, or it's gone forever.

He thought about a kid back at Madison Junior College, where he coached for a short spell. The kid was a running back who always carried the football low on his hip. Charlie coached him to carry the ball up high, in his armpit, but the kid always forgot. On two occasions during important games he fumbled the ball because of the way he toted the thing. When reminded he'd always reply, "Oh, yeah, right. I forgot."

That's where Charlie stumbled across a simple way to magnify his learning technique: if you really want something to stick in your mind, share it out loud twice in one day, consciously, purposefully, intentionally. He told that running back to share, twice a day, the importance of carrying the ball high. Tell anyone. Preach it, yell it, write it, tattoo it—twice a day to anyone for any reason. That way he'd never forget.

He picked up his laptop and shot off a quick email to Picasso. Charlie wasn't a rah-rah guy so the encouragement felt clumsy. It just said, "I'm not giving up. I'm an all-day sucker." It was just a quick thought. A shot in the dark really. But sometimes those little ideas find their mark. Then again he really wasn't sending it for Picasso; he was sending it for himself.

Lisa walked back into the room with her vitals cart and another note.

"I'm not quittin'. I'm an all-day sucker," Charlie said, his second out-loud touch of the day.

Lisa's eyes widened and her face broke into a smile. Touched. Shocked really. Mean old Charlie saying something nice?

"Bring it all day, sucka!" she shot back, rocking her head

in that playful way. "Those words mean a lot coming from you, Coach. Glad to see your spirits are up. Got another letter for you, but this one is a little different."

She put down the tray and handed a beat-up letter to Charlie. It had no stamp, a scribbled address, and his name was misspelled. It looked like a kid had written it. The return address seemed to say "Max, 3rd floor, UAB Cancer Hospital."

He smiled a bit, wondering what this was all about. He opened the letter wondering if this was some sort of practical joke.

Dear Coach Cristo, it began. *I am your biggest fan. I grew up in Seminole Valley, Alabama, watching the Seminole Valley Bucks. I think they are great. I found out that you had to stop coaching because you have cancer. You have the same cancer I have. I thought I would send you a note and cheer you up.*

The writing was shaky and hard to decipher. It was clearly a kid, a young kid, probably writing from a bed like Charlie's.

An old, dark reaction popped up in Charlie. *Kid probably wants an autograph or tickets or a picture with his dad or something*, he thought.

He stopped himself. The note had sincerity and inno-cence. He shifted in his bed. He felt himself thaw a degree or two. Better, not bitter. He relaxed and opened his mind.

I want to give you some free advice. Your defense needs some work. You have some hard tacklers but they drink too much water on the sidelines.

Charlie smiled, melting a bit on the inside. He'd have to keep an eye on that water business.

Also, I think you will find that the nurses are nicer if you are nice to them first. I tried it and it really works good.

Charlie cracked another smile. He found himself gently hooked. The kid was getting to him.

And one more thing. My throat gets real sore. I found out that strawberry Popsicles are very good for the pain. Eat lots and lots and lots of them. They are free. The nurses like me so I think that's why they don't make me pay money. I have to go now but I'll write again later. I hope I can play for you someday. Bye for now.

Your biggest fan, Max.

Well, that was a complete surprise. Who was this kid? For a clear and fresh moment Charlie was completely immersed in something else. He felt an instant connection to someone facing the same dark and difficult race with death. A kid no less, fighting cancer with candor and courage. An all-day sucker. Those moments of connection were so rare, and better than drugs. Charlie was deeply intrigued. He'd find this kid.

THE NEXT DAY Charlie was released to go home for a week's worth of R & R. When Eve arrived promptly at nine, Charlie was up and ready. He'd assembled what few things he had in a small suitcase. On top of the suitcase was the old shoebox and a small spiral notebook. Eve was familiar with that box, but she was under the impression that Charlie could care less about the contents. It surprised her to see them carefully arranged.

"I thought you didn't want anything to do with those letters," she said.

"I read a few and they're not what I thought. There's some good stuff in there."

"Umm . . . okay," she replied. "What's in the notebook?"

"It's blank now, but I'm going to start writing some things in later. I'll show you. Before we go home can we run by the UAB Pediatric Cancer Center? There is someone there I want to see."

"Uh, sure we can go there. Who do you have to see?"

"Someone I want us both to meet. I'll tell you in the car."

A nurse put Charlie in a wheelchair, piled his few possessions in his lap, and Eve slapped a new Seminole Valley Bucks ball cap on his head, and out the door they went to the elevator.

Soon they were in the car, heading to the pediatric unit of the UAB Comprehensive Cancer Center. The sun, the air, the sounds . . . it was wonderful and Charlie absorbed every second like it was his first time being outside. Just being outside was intoxicating. Everything was moving. It seemed so strange to him, yet oddly absorbing.

Eve had asked him several questions but he gave little more than mumbled answers.

"Are you going to tell me about who we are meeting?" Eve asked.

"Got a letter from a kid. His name is Max. He has leukemia like mine. He seemed like a good kid, and I just wanted to meet him. I hope you don't mind."

He knew she did mind. "It's fine," she replied with just the right amount of pout. Her passive-aggressiveness was surgical.

Charlie felt a sudden and sharp sense of exhaustion sweep over him. He began second-guessing the wisdom of this visit to Max, but he kept it to himself.

He figured they'd have the best chance of finding this kid in the children's cancer wing if they arrived just before lunch.

They entered the hospital and approached the main desk. Charlie was walking very slowly, thinking about that pathetically straggly and haggard guy he just saw walk by in the lobby mirror. He was used to seeing a former Heisman candidate strolling along, shoulders back, head high, gut washboard flat. Instead he saw a gray, scrawny, limping cadaver.

The receptionist put her call on hold and told them the ER was around the corner.

Ouch, Charlie thought. Did he look that bad to others? He felt bad for Eve. Could anyone help the beautiful woman and her sick, zombie husband?

The receptionist apologized repeatedly when informed of her misread, but Charlie put her at ease.

"No need all of us feeling miserable," Charlie said to assure her.

"Who are you looking for?" the receptionist asked Charlie kindly when told of his desire to see a patient.

"I know this is a huge hospital and you have a lot of patients. I hope you can help. I don't know his last name, but he's a kid and his name is Max."

The receptionist broke into a broad smile.

"Honey, everyone here knows Max!" Beaming, she picked up the phone.

"Visitor here to see Max," she began. "Can he take guests today?" She listened quietly to a nurse on the other end, then said thank you and hung up.

"He's a little tired today. He has good days and bad days, like all of us. But he can see you for a little bit."

Charlie knew all about it.

The receptionist smiled and whispered, "He'd love to see you. He loves seeing everyone. His nurses are just a little *overprotective . . .*"

Charlie and Eve thanked her and followed her directions to the third floor.

PEDIATRIC CANCER WARDS are different than the wards for adults. They are brightly colored, energetic and uplifting. They reflect a celebration of life. And the nursing staff is cut from a different cloth. There is a *spirit* among them. They fight for a mighty cause and bring with them a razor-sharp, can-do edge slicing through fear and hopelessness. It's an uncanny, never-say-never, do-it-or-die-trying attitude that fills their tiny patients with hope and possibility. These professionals would never quit on anyone, especially kids. Failure is clearly not an option. Young lives *will* be saved. It's a cause worth believing in and being excited about.

Despite his growing exhaustion, Charlie was immediately energized. For the first time in ages, deep down, he felt like he had something of value to offer here. Football was great, but this was life.

Or death. Beneath the laughter, color, flowers, slogans and sweet songs lurked something very real and gritty and deeply scary. He recognized it in the twenty or so bald, concerned, and vulnerable kids who turned to look at him and Eve as they entered. Charlie felt a visceral connection, and feared none of it.

A hawk-eyed nurse named Sharona escorted them to Max's room. Max was the crown jewel; Sharona the compassionate but no-nonsense sentinel. She made it clear that *nobody* was going to stay very long. She reminded Charlie of a Secret Service agent—Max had had a bad week and they were guarding him.

Charlie removed his new hat and stuffed it under his arm as he walked into the room.

"Max, you have some visitors," the nurse said quietly as they entered together.

The sight of Max in bed was difficult, even for a fellow cancer fighter. Young Max was smallish, probably about ten years old though it was hard to tell. He was reed thin, and seemed to be covered in tubes. The room had the unmistakable scent of cancer chemicals, and the lights were low. First glance suggested Max was sleeping, but when he heard the group enter the room he alerted and did his best to sit up.

His eyes sparkled for someone in his condition. He licked his lips over and over as if to force some moisture in so he could speak. Charlie connected with that immediately.

"Hey, little man," Charlie spoke quietly, coming alongside the bed.

The first words out of Max's mouth—"Wanna rub my head?"—shocked both of them, and Charlie and Eve shot glances back and forth.

"Don't be afraid," he continued, "it's for luck."

Charlie smiled at the thought. Like rubbing the Buddha's belly at a Chinese restaurant. He reached out and touched the boy's bald scalp. Then he held his hand on Max's little head and squeezed gently. Eve did the same. A lifelong bond formed in just a second.

"I never thought about doing that," Charlie said, reaching up to rub his own hairless head. "All this time a skinhead and I never did anything but complain."

"Who are you?" Max asked.

"My name is Charlie Cristo and I coach the Seminole Valley Bucks. Remember you sent me a note not long ago?"

Max's mouth dropped open slightly.

"You're famous," he said, eyes widening. "I don't know anyone famous, though sometimes people like talking to me. I guess that makes me sorta famous."

Charlie and Eve chuckled.

As they continued to talk, Charlie sensed that Max was bright and insightful. He was pretty talkative too. Charlie was used to communicating with football players. This was a respite.

"I heard all your players shaved their heads for you when you went in for your treatment," Max said.

"Yeah, they did. It was very nice of them. But the best thing for me was that great letter you sent me. You gave me some solid football advice."

Max sat up slightly and began frantically licking his lips as if he wanted to speak but couldn't get the words past the dryness. Eve quickly reached for a blue water jug and Max took a long, satisfying drag on the straw.

"That's better" Max said. "I hope the advice helps." A drop of water rolled down his chin. Eve moved quickly to dab it but Max caught it with a quick flick of his arm. He continued without distraction.

"I don't coach but I love watching your team. My Grampy says you really know what you're doing. He keeps saying 'great defense, *GREAT* defense!'" Max's eyes lit up with excitement, reliving some moment in his memory.

"Well, we had a rough start, Max. Those guys have turned it around since the first couple of games, but it's been a fight."

"I think Grampy was talking about how good you are, not what the score was."

Good line, Charlie thought. Perceptive kid.

"Who is your Grampy?"

"They're Max's guardians . . . Grammy and Grampy," Sharona said out of nowhere.

"Yeah, my mom and dad are gone," Max said, apparently unaware of any peculiarity. "Grammy and Grampy have raised me for as long as I know. They love football."

"They sound like great people," Charlie added. "Someday maybe we can meet."

"My Grampy would love to meet a star like you."

Charlie felt strangely humbled.

"Do you mind if I have a Popsicle?" Max asked politely. "It helps my lips stay wet."

"Sure, sure, yes!" Charlie and Eve burst out almost in unison.

The nurse, Sharona, opened a small refrigerator and pulled out a strawberry Popsicle for Max. His favorite. As she handed it to him he asked if his guests might have some too. Sharona reached in the fridge again and got two more, not saying a word.

"How are you feeling today?" Eve asked Max.

He looked at his Popsicle, then at Eve, then back at the Popsicle and took another bite, never answering the question. It was a dangling moment. Awkward. Then Charlie came to the rescue.

"I've had a lot of long, painful, and sad days, Max. I know what you must be going through."

Max brightened. "You don't have to be sad, Charlie; you have me now. We'll fight together."

Charlie winced and forced a smile, trying to keep it together in the face of an immense wave of emotion coming up from somewhere. Eve looked like she wanted to scoop up Max and hold him.

The thought struck him how wonderful it would be to have players with this kind of heart, inner strength, and honesty.

Then another thought in fast succession: maybe, if Max felt well enough, Charlie could take him along to the pregame pep talk he promised the team he would make during his break. He was speaking to the team on Friday afternoon.

Brilliant. It would be great for everyone.

"We know you're tired today, Max. I get tired all the time too. So maybe we can come back and see you soon. Maybe I could bring some players back with me, or maybe you could go with me to the locker room sometime if you felt like it."

Max bolted upright, summoning an energy surge that shocked everyone. His eyes were wide and beaming.

"Would you do *that*?" His thin voice stretched. For an

instant he was just a little kid with the biggest fan heart in the world.

"I'll have to check with your nurse," Charlie said, deferring to the authority present, "and then we'll see."

Max was irrepressible. He squirmed and smiled and began fiddling with his fingers. He could hardly contain his sudden surge of excitement.

"Everywhere I go I find such nice people!" Max said through dry and cracked, grinning lips. "I'm so happy I sent you that advice letter."

Charlie's mind lit with another sudden thought.

"I would like to send you some letters too, if I could. I get letters from a good friend of mine that you might like. I have a whole box of them. Maybe you would like to read some?"

Max couldn't stop beaming and suddenly began squirming around . . . like a little kid. "Yes!"

Charlie glanced at Eve. He imagined she was thinking, *Charlie, send a letter?* He knew she was right, and resolved to follow through.

Eve was also instantly interested in the letters. Charlie had spoken little of them before, and when he did it was always with skepticism or derision.

"Good," Charlie said. "Before I go I have something I want you to have."

Charlie reached down and picked up the Seminole Valley Bucks hat he'd received from Eve. He resized it and put it on Max's head. It was big, and covered Max's ears.

Max grinned away, his thin skin stretching across his small, bony face. None of them wanted the moment to end.

They said their good-byes and Charlie promised to check back later in the week to see how Max was doing. Maybe he'd be well enough to travel to Seminole Valley on Friday.

They hugged and made for the door. Then Max blurted something that stopped the whole group in their tracks.

"I'm strong if you're strong, Charlie. Are you strong?"

Charlie turned back toward Max and froze, seized by the comment, unsure what to say.

"Excuse me?" he said, cocking his head slightly, amazed at the wisdom that just bubbled out of this little character.

"I'm strong if you're strong. Are you strong? You're supposed to say 'I'm strong' real loud," Max replied.

Nobody spoke. Everyone looked at Max, then at one another, each feeling something special in the air, binding them all together in some way.

"I'm strong," Charlie said after a long and thoughtful pause.

"It was in a letter one of the nurses gave me," Max said.

"In a letter?" Charlie replied, suddenly curious.

"Yeah. It's right here."

Max lifted up a beat-up, crayon-marked envelope lying next to his bed. One of Charlie's letters had somehow found its way into Max's possession.

Charlie stared, shocked and speechless. *How did this happen?* He remembered giving away some of those early letters to Bing, but never in his wildest imagination . . .

So he smiled. He had no idea what was in this letter, but Max had already mastered it. He wondered how many more were floating around out there.

"I think this is addressed to you, but a nice nurse gave it to me because I can read pretty good . . ."

Charlie flushed and was choked with astonishment.

Then he swallowed hard and replied, "I'm strong if you're strong, Max. Are you strong?"

"I'm strong, Coach!" Max yelled, collapsing suddenly into a quiet coughing spell of his own.

"Yes you are, my little man, yes you are," Charlie said quietly to himself as he reached forward and gently squeezed Max's head, covered now by a Seminole Bucks ball cap.

He asked Max if me might take the letter and learn some of the lessons for himself. Max nodded his head with gusto and handed it to Charlie. As Charlie reached for it their hands touched. Max's skin was warm and alive. Max looked at Charlie and said simply, "Oh, please take this, Coach, I'm strong."

Charlie never had any boys of his own. He'd always wondered what it would be like. In that moment he realized that sometimes you have sons, and sometimes sons just show up.

They got Max settled down, bid their good-byes, and left the room. Once outside Charlie took the nurse aside and asked to have the blanks of Max's life filled in. What she'd just witnessed warmed her considerably and she told him what she could about Max's condition without breaking any rules. As it turns out he was very ill. They could not get his vitals stabilized; yet on certain days he seemed perfectly normal and healthy. He was much loved on the floor and had become a favorite of the staff. His grandparents were raising him. His real parents were drug addicted and long gone. Orphaned, but thank God not alone.

Charlie asked again about coming out for the pep talk on Friday. To sweeten the deal he asked Sharona to come as well. He hoped this gesture would help make it happen. It worked. It turns out Sharona was a football fan too.

"I won't be allowed to do that, but thanks for asking. Call the ward on Friday morning, Coach," she replied. "If Max's well, I'll see if I can find a professional chaperone or perhaps a family member who could go with him. It would really help his spirits I'm sure."

"Honestly, it would really help ours," Charlie replied.

They departed, turning to look one last time into Max's room. He was fast asleep. Charlie smiled.

As he and Eve approached the car to go home, he noticed her holding back tears. He didn't need to ask. He felt the same way.

They got in the car and Charlie put Max's letter in the glove box for safekeeping.

They were quiet for a long time. Finally gathering herself, Eve spoke.

"I want you to tell me more about these letters, Charlie. Could I see some?"

Charlie, still somewhat ashamed about the careless way he'd handled them in the first place, gladly agreed.

"They're pretty good," he said.

"They'd have to be," she replied.

CHARLIE HAD NOT BEEN together with Eve and the girls for some time. Since Charlie had gone into the hospital Eve and the girls had settled into a rhythm in the house. They all seemed happy there. Charlie loved the drive up the street of his home and looked forward to a break from the cancer ward and a week of something close to normal. He was exhausted as they drove into the driveway. He never expected what was waiting.

Standing on his lawn with "Welcome Home, Coach!" signs were his four co-captains and acting head coach Picasso. Charlie felt fatherly pride for these guys: Andrew Martinez, his quarterback; Jonathon Ranger, a running back; and Scotty "Bobby" Bouche and Winston "Axle" Johnson, linebackers and star players. He was so proud and so touched that he literally broke down crying as he exited the car. The boys and Coach Picasso looked at one another, then encircled Charlie as he leaned against the car sobbing. The floodgates of emotion suddenly opened and Charlie could not turn it off. The kindness of their gesture hit the chink in his emotional armor. He thanked them over and over again, helplessly blubbering and unapologetic.

In a few moments he'd gathered himself and they made their way to the front porch and all sat down. It was a thrill to be with those guys again. Charlie basked in their energy and imagination as they told him story after story of how, inspired by the comeback story of their coach, they stormed back from their bad 1–2 start to the current 4–2 record. A three-game run. They looked unstoppable. A few more weeks of this and they'd make the state playoffs. Football was religion in Alabama, and winning state was getting to heaven.

"We're excited to have you come and talk to us this week, Coach," Andrew reminded Charlie. All the players nodded in agreement. "This is a huge game for us. Get by these guys and we'll have a clear shot at the post season. Your words will mean the world to us, Coach."

Charlie felt electrified. He thanked the boys, then shifted the conversation to what they were doing to win, if they'd used any of the plays he suggested, how practices were going, any update on injuries, and so on. He especially wanted to know if any of his leaders thought the guys drank too much water on the sidelines. The captains all looked at each other and snickered.

"All right, guys, don't laugh. I had to ask. Someone mentioned that so I thought I should ask." Talking football with his boys was the second best thing to happen to him in weeks.

Charlie thought the boys must see nothing but a frail, gray shell of a man. But he was different, and he knew it. He hoped they would see there was something better about him, a sort of thoughtfulness or something they didn't quite recognize. He imagined they would talk about it later and conclude that hard-guy Charlie Cristo must be worn out from the chemo. No way was *that* guy changing, they'd say.

Little did they know.

The group of them sat on the porch talking football philosophy, how to make the team more effective, personnel packages, special teams play, and more. Nirvana for Charlie.

Within about a half hour he'd hit the final wall. He slowly and politely asked the boys if he could just rest up a bit before they spoke further. Somewhat embarrassed that they'd overstayed their welcome, they told him they'd head out. Charlie was crestfallen that they'd taken his words that way, but too late. They hugged their coach, encouraged him, and said they'd look forward to one of his rousing pep talks on Friday.

"Okay, boys, but," he added, "I might be bringing a special guest with me. I want you to meet this guy. His name is Max, and I think you'll like him." The boys were their typical selves at the news: enthused and ready to welcome any friend of the coach.

Charlie was deeply grateful as the boys and Coach Picasso drove off that afternoon.

I've gotta bring something special for those guys Friday night, he thought.

That evening at home was special for Charlie, Eve, and the girls. For the first time in what seemed to be ages they all ate together, talked, laughed, and joked. Charlie missed his girls. Now here his family was, together again, all four of them.

Charlie caught up with Jen and Jess, listening to their stories of their new school, boys, sports, and grades. Jess was a freshman and Jen a sophomore at Seminole Valley, and quasi-stars since their dad was the new head coach . . . and famously ill.

Charlie paid attention to them like he'd never done before. He listened to them without judgment or preoccupation with other things. He listened to them like it was the first time ever. He fell in love with them all over again.

And Eve. They hadn't spent a great deal of "normal" time together since their difficult split, his move to Alabama, and his sickness. He felt in some ways as though he didn't even know her. Yet here they all were laughing, teasing, and catching up. It felt so normal, so perfectly wonderful. If he didn't know this woman before, he wanted to now. Before it was too late.

But it might be too late. The thought stuck his heart like a dagger. Charlie felt the sudden emergence of the dark cloud hanging over their marriage and his life. He fell quiet. He couldn't hide it. Everyone at the table noticed.

"What's the matter, Dad?" Jessie asked.

"Just . . . thinking. Worrying a little bit, I guess," he replied.

The table became deafeningly silent as everyone realized it was time to talk about the elephant in the room.

Charlie's meager appetite disappeared.

"I'm sick, girls. You know that. They tell me that round two of chemo is the worst. I don't know if I can make it. Round one was more horrible than I can say. I'm afraid this will kill me. And you know what bothers me the most?"

Nobody breathed.

"What bothers me the most is the thought that I couldn't dance at your weddings."

The girls looked down and said nothing. Then Jen lifted her head, glaring.

"Dad. You are *going* to dance at our weddings. We're gonna *make you*. You might be skinny and you might be bald, but you're gonna dance. No excuses. That's what you always taught us, right? No excuses! We're *CRISTOs*, Daddy! Cristos don't quit!"

Charlie's eyes pricked with tears. They'd remembered his famous "No excuses" rule. All his girls looked at him and smiled. Strained and fearful, yet hopeful, smiles.

THE WEEK FLEW BY. It was a wonderful break from the rigors of hospital life. It was as close to normal as Charlie had felt in years. Before he knew it, it was Thursday night; time to get ready for his big pep talk the next afternoon. As if the aftereffects of the chemo weren't bad enough, pep talks always taxed Charlie. He was like most coaches this way: if anything could be or needed to be said, he'd long since said it. What could he bring that was new? Fresh? Inspiring?

He was just too physically and emotionally sapped to think too hard about it. He lay staring out his bedroom window, imagining himself speaking to his warriors. The boys had managed to win every contest since he'd left. In all honesty he thought that perhaps he should be asking *them* what needed to be said. They were the ones who'd rallied themselves to pull off the wins.

Then again, the coaches reminded him that his sickness had galvanized the boys. They'd gone from being kids playing a game to a team of young fighters on a mission. The coaches were unanimous in their opinion that the boys had somehow managed to weld themselves into one mind and one heart. Charlie and his battle were all they talked about. Charlie was astonished and proud of them beyond words.

He needed to say something that could maybe match their passion for his situation. For reasons he could not pinpoint, he'd been having a solitary thought clattering around in his head. He couldn't identify the cause or the source, but it kept coming back—not totally formed, and nothing he could share yet, but nevertheless in there. Then it struck him that perhaps there would be something in that box of letters that would help in his talk. Surely there would be.

He found the box of letters and began going through the unopened notes. They were great. The more he read them, the more inspired he became. The more inspired he became, the more certain he grew that he would have the perfect words for his boys.

Then he found the one: the perfect letter and the perfect way to use it. He'd call Max in the morning; God willing, the kid would be well enough to go along.

Charlie slept soundly that night. For the first time in months, he dreamed.

CHAPTER .11

THE MORNING PASSED QUICKLY as Charlie planned his afternoon. He'd called the hospital first thing to verify that Max was in good shape. He spoke to Sharona, who suggested Grampy join them. Charlie gladly agreed.

At one o'clock he was ready to go. Eve came into the garage to leave and saw that Charlie had pulled out two coolers and was loading them in the trunk of the car.

"What are you doing?" she asked.

"Surprise for the boys. We need to stop at the store and get some ice."

Eve seemed to notice Charlie's energy and excitement. Of course, nothing much seemed to excite him these days, he knew that. If that's all it took to make her smile, he'd try a little harder.

On the way to the hospital they stopped at the supermarket and Charlie went in. Eve asked if she could help but Charlie declined with a mischievous glint in his eye. Sure, he was moving slow, but he asked two young guys standing nearby to help him carry in the coolers. He returned to the car ten minutes later with the two guys carrying the now-full coolers.

Charlie *hopped* back in the car. Whatever he was up to had juiced him, at least for the moment.

A short drive later they were entering the patient pick-up driveway at the UAB Cancer Center. Max, wearing his Seminole Valley hat, was sitting in a wheelchair next to an old man on a bench.

Sharona was nowhere. As Eve and Charlie pulled up, the old man approached the car.

"Hi, Mr. Cristo. I'm Ollie, Max's grandpa, but everyone calls me Grampy. Sharona suggested I go with you this afternoon. Is that okay?"

Charlie was moved.

"Of course, Grampy. Glad to have you along."

Max was sitting in his chair fist-pumping the air. It was a moment of instant camaraderie.

Together with Eve, they helped Max in the car and headed to the high school.

"Where is Sharona, Max?" Charlie asked.

Max burst into the chorus of the old rock 'n' roll classic, "My Sharona." Hysterics erupted. Everyone was thinking the same thing.

"I guess you heard about that song, huh?" teased Charlie.

"Everyone on the floor sings it for her. She has famous ways and told us the song is about her. She likes to dance for us when nobody is looking."

This kid could say the funniest things. And he seemed to feel pretty good this afternoon. His energy seemed to peak as Ollie and Charlie talked about the old days when Charlie quarterbacked the Tide. Max and Ollie had never been around someone they considered a celebrity. Eve just smiled and listened to the two guys and Max talk. She hadn't seen Charlie relish a moment like this in a long time.

They arrived at Seminole Valley High at the beginning of the afternoon pep assembly. They pulled around to the back by the locker rooms. There was a buzz in the air about that night's game. Everyone could feel it. The banners, the sound of kids cheering in the gym, the band playing, the field decked out, and media trucks and venders assembling everywhere.

And school wasn't even out yet. It was an atmosphere and ritual that Charlie loved. Game day was the same every week: the team would wear their jerseys, the school would be festooned with signs, posters, and streamers, the staff would be energized, and the place would have been rocking since the first bell. Especially since the team appeared to be bona fide winners. The last period of the school day the kids would meet in the gym for a climactic pep rally. Sure, this was probably the same in schools across the country, but theirs just seemed better. Everybody needs something to be excited about.

The pep rally would be starting momentarily, and Charlie had been asked to share a few words before his talk to the team. The four were greeted by the principal, athletic director, and two coaches as they exited the car. They exchanged hearty greetings and introduced everyone all around. Max in his excitement pulled out a pen and an old envelope and started asking everyone for autographs. Embarrassed chuckles and sheepish signing followed, and everyone was duly flattered. Max was beside himself.

As they walked into the building, Max turned to Charlie.

"Are you nervous?" he quizzed.

Charlie slowed a bit and thought.

"Yeah. Yeah, Max I'm nervous. I do not like talking in front of huge crowds. Football teams, yes. Big crowds, no way."

"Can I give you some advice? Something good to say?" Max offered.

"Sure can. What'cha got?"

Max pulled up close to Charlie and waved him down, closer. Then he whispered something in Charlie's ear. Charlie cracked up laughing.

"You got it, buddy. I just might use that!"

As they entered the building, everything went into a much higher gear. The place was mad with activity. They could hear the entire band playing in the gym as the floor rumbled. Classes had just been dismissed and kids were presently streaming into the large hall. The atmosphere was electric.

As they entered the cavernous gym, the drums pounded, cheers were screamed, and kids jammed and crammed, joked and jostled in the stands. The principal called the assembly to order, but none of the students heard. They only grew louder. The deafening cheers continued as the co-captains of the team, the coaching staff, and athletic trainers were introduced. Each shared short, rousing words that could barely be heard in the din.

Then came Charlie's moment. He was introduced and he slowly moved to the podium in the middle of the basketball court. The screams and clapping were magnified by the emotion, the climax of the moment. Eve helped Charlie as he moved slowly forward. Max, agog at the spectacle, held his ears and whooped nonstop in unison with the crowd.

Grampy stood by his side looking upward and grinning, lost in amazement.

Charlie, thin and ashen, straightened himself as best he could and stepped up to the podium. He hadn't thought much about what he would say to the *whole school*, and he was completely overwhelmed by this reception. He immediately teared up at the flood of love from those kids. He couldn't stop the faucets in his eyes. The pandemonium only grew as the entire school gave him a standing ovation.

Finally the crowd quieted, and Charlie gathered himself.

"I came today to speak to the team, and I'm honored to also be speaking to you guys. I don't know what to say; you've all left me speechless with your kindness and cheers."

Charlie's voice was raspy and strained. The crowd started cheering again, then quickly grew quiet, sensing that Charlie had only limited energy.

Charlie stood quietly with really no idea what to say. Then out of nowhere a thought struck. It was one that had been rattling around in his head for days.

"I'm not good at this and honestly, I'm scared. I want to tell you something I've learned while I've been in chemo. I just can't seem to shake this out of my mind, and I hope it sticks with you too. I'm really not here today to talk about football, though tonight's game is huge. And I'm not here to talk about cancer. That disease speaks for itself. I'm here to talk about life. *Your life*. Cancer has a way of prioritizing the clutter in your mind and focusing you on what's important. Imagine if tomorrow you went to the doctor and they told you to forget all your dreams. You've got cancer now and your life is in eminent danger. Forget whatever job or career you have or hope you're going to have. Forget your big dreams of being free and maybe going on to college or the military or just working. Forget it all. None of them are going to happen. You just have one job, *stay alive*, and there are no guarantees. Trust me, that news would change you instantly."

Charlie was quiet for a moment, collecting his thoughts. The audience was silent.

"When they told me I had cancer a couple months ago, I first thought they were kidding. I had so much to do, so much to live for, so much ahead of me. Then all of a sudden . . . blackness. Nothing. Just me and my dreadful future. To tell you the truth, I went home and cried. I was scared, alone, and my whole world was wiped away. No vision, no hope, no nothin'.

"But you know what I learned very early in all that? I learned a very cold truth: *cancer don't care*." Charlie emphasized the words with three jabs of his forefinger, then sighed and let his hand drop. "Cancer doesn't care what my dreams or aspirations are. It doesn't care if I beat it or not.

It doesn't care if I live or die. It just doesn't care. So let me give you some advice: *you better care*. I'm not speaking to you as a coach, a teacher, your dad, an elder, or a wise guy . . . just as a friend. Your friend. Get after your dreams now. Don't wait. Don't blame your circumstances. Don't doubt yourself. Don't talk yourself out of it. No, take action now . . . because cancer doesn't care. Get going and live your life no matter what you may be up against. Approach it with grit, because quitting ain't allowed, and cancer don't care. *You* gotta care with all your heart. Commit to something good and don't quit on it. Do something good. Please do yourself a favor and do something good."

The kids were stone-cold still. When a dead man talks, people listen.

"I'm not done with this yet. Two more courses of chemo that they say are worse than the first. Am I scared? Yes. Am I going to make it? Cancer don't care, so I decided one of us better. So yes, I'm going to make it. You know why? And I'm not kidding when I say this: *it's because people love me.* They encourage me, they stand by me, they yell at me, they cry with me, they tell me to have grit, and they kick my butt when I need it.

"Sorry about the language kids, but this is real. And I needed it. And they loved me and would never leave me.

And I count you among those who love me. Thank you from the bottom of my heart. I will survive this because I have you, and you love me. I know it."

Spontaneous applause built into a rousing ovation.

Charlie took a deep breath. "Now," Charlie continued, "let's talk about our game tonight!"

The crowd detonated. Charlie waited for the reverberation to settle down.

"They're a tough team," he began, "but the Bucks are a gritty team. We're a gritty team because we fight for something bigger than ourselves . . . we fight for each other. We love each other, and we, all of us here in this auditorium, rely on each other to be our strongest. So show up tonight and support your brothers. You, me, them . . . us . . . we're in this together and we need your support. Will you join us?"

The place went mad-dog nuts, with students screaming and yelling, jumping up and down, stamping their feet and pounding anything that didn't pound back. It was perfection.

Then Charlie caved the house in. Motioning Max forward, he asked the crowd to quiet then introduced the smallish, sickly little boy with a big grin and a Seminole Valley Bucks hat tucked over his ears.

"This is my friend Max and he gave me some advice that I want you all to hear. It sums it all up. Tell them what you told me, Max."

Max moved to the mic shyly, then, flashing his incandescent grin, yelled, "Just win, baby!"

They moved away from the rattling podium as cheers echoed off the walls and the ground went seismic. They could feel it as they moved back into the locker rooms.

THE GAME DID NOT officially begin till seven, but on game day the players stayed around for a pregame meal at four, then some kick-back time, and then pregame suit-up and warm-up at six. Coach Cristo was scheduled to talk to them at five.

Talking to the students had exhausted him much more than he'd thought it would. Nevertheless he rallied himself and felt ready to go as five o'clock neared. He'd spent some time with his players and felt so at home. Everyone was unbelievably kind and encouraging. He missed the locker room and his team more than he could say.

Max was getting along fine with the boys as well. They'd found him a wheelchair and were taking turns running him around the hallways. Grampy stood in the background and watched with pleasure. And the players loved signing autographs for Max and regaling him with stories of "big-time football." Max loved all of it, and the boys loved the little man.

It was pep talk time. The players came to attention as Coach Picasso blew a whistle, clapped his hands and brought the guys together. "Coach!" he said.

Charlie had been meeting with the assistants and the captains for about an hour and his energy was sapped, but not his enthusiasm. He had enough left in the tank for the talk, but that was about it. He wasted no time in going to the front of the locker room, where Picasso introduced him.

"Men," Charlie began, "it's almost beyond me that I could even be here speaking before you right now. But miracles happen . . . and look at me!" he said, playfully flexing his bony arms. The players laughed lightly and gave their coach warm applause.

"I've spent the last few weeks lying in a bed fighting an enemy I can't even see. There have been some victories and some setbacks. I would never want you guys to see how I acted or what I said to myself most of the time, because I have to admit many of those days I was losing the game. But the good news is that I'm here, I'm happy to be here, and now I'm winning this fight."

The boys' applause surged for their champion. Their claps turned into hooting and banging the lockers. Max sat up front covering his ears, a little intimidated by the emotion and sound and the sheer size of the players.

"I want to tell you that I learned something about cancer that will help you in your game tonight."

Remembering some lines from a recent letter, Charlie continued.

"What I learned from cancer is that as long as you keep fighting, *the game will let you stick around*. What happens with cancer, the way it beats you is it pushes you to the point where you don't feel like fighting anymore. You get so tired and you just don't want to stick around. You get whipped and you walk away. It's how cancer beats you. You just don't feel like fighting anymore.

"So what keeps you fighting? What keeps you sticking around? It's when you know that people love you. When you have cancer and know that people love you, you think, *Cancer, come on, come on. Bring it on.* When I recall the way my wife and my family love me, I think, *Cancer, come on. I'm sticking around. C'mon!* When I watched video today of the way you guys have played while I've been gone, I think, *Cancer, come on, come on. You bring it.*

"When I watched the way you, Axle, when I watched the way you anchored the defense and led this team, for me, I say, *Cancer, come on. You just bring it. I got you!* Andrew, when I watched the way you went out there and played, with that kind of spirit and that kind of heart and the way all of you guys—you linemen—help him, protect him . . . *Cancer, you just come on. You come on!*

"Picasso, my man, the way you unselfishly picked up for me and did everything for me. The way you coach. *Come on, cancer, you just come on!*"

The boys were starting to move restlessly, like race horses in the gate, bubbling with the energy that precedes an explosion.

"It's the love of others. That what's makes you stick around. That's what it comes down to. That's how you take on cancer. You stick around. That's how you win state football championships. You stick around. I'm asking you to go play today because you love each other. Because if loving your fellow players like you loved me makes them stick around like it did for me, *no one has a chance* against you guys. Nobody! Not these guys we're playing tonight, not anybody! *Cancer, come on!* Keep sticking around, boys. All night. Every play. I love you guys. Thanks for everything you've done for me. I'll never forget it."

The boys got the message. Charlie did one more thing to seal it.

"Before I go I want to tell you something I learned from a very special person. You've all met Max over there, right?"

The boys all nodded and looked at Max, turning red

as he sat next to co-captain Bobby Bouche on a bench up front.

"Max taught me that when you don't feel good or you're worried, eat a Popsicle. It makes your throat feel better, then you get better."

On cue, several of the players dragged in the two coolers Charlie brought with him. Charlie motioned to Max to come forward, and he ceremoniously opened them both. They were filled with Popsicles.

"Everyone take one," Charlie said. "And when you're done, take the stick and carry it with you into battle tonight. Your opponents tonight don't know it, but you guys are going to stick around for the whole game. No matter what happens, stick around. Cancer lets you stick around; that's how you beat it. This team tonight will let you stick around too . . . that's how you beat them. On behalf of Max, stick around tonight and win it."

Nobody could tell what happened next. It was a blur. Max was mobbed, and the boys made him the honorary "Buck" for the game. It was a happy mess, and win number five was in the cards for the resurging, and loving, Seminole Valley Bucks.

CHAPTER .13

CHARLIE HAD A GOOD WEEKEND. The boys won their ball game 32–14 and were now 5–2. They were right on track for the playoffs. Charlie was back with his girls, and perhaps most surprising, he had a close new charge in his life: Max. Life was suddenly good.

Charlie turned his attention to prepping for what was coming on Monday. He found a letter that really helped.

Hi, Charlie.

Taking it higher. This is the mind-set for your second round of chemo.

I spoke in New York City yesterday. And you hear all kinds of rumors about New York City but to be honest with you, they are my best crowds.

So I had a guy up front, an older gentlemen. He had a cane. And he was very curmudgeonly. He decided he was going to yell stuff at me. One time he yelled at me, "You don't know anything!" And finally the crowd shushed him and he left.

I was thinking maybe I dated his daughter a long time ago. But I did not go down and choke him; I didn't even get the urge to. Look, I'm no superman. I'm human. I have an ego, unfortunately, I have to surrender every day to God. But why didn't I have the urge to yell back?

Then I figured out why it didn't bother me: I didn't come there for their approval. No, I came there to give them the best talk I knew how to give; a talk I felt they needed to hear. And that was even more important to me than their approval. It allowed me to rise above it, to take it higher.

Right about now you are going in for your second round of chemo. Go higher. When you feel something gnawing at you, when chemo says, "Take that," or when chemo says to you, "You don't know anything, feel this," go higher. You know how I was there to give them the best talk I could? You are there to get healthy. Nothing else matters. Go higher. Visualize health. Visualize your body being restored. When that comes, just keep on telling yourself, I'm going higher.

I don't know why that guy didn't bother me when I was talking. I think it was because I was shooting for something higher.

This has become my recent favorite story so I've probably told it to you before. Here goes again. Nelson Mandela walked out of prison and years later he invited his jailer to his inaguration. He was telling President Bill Clinton this story. And Clinton asked him if he hated the men who imprisoned him. Mandela said for a moment he was very angry. But he thought, "Nelson, if you continue to hate them, you will still be their prisoner." Go higher.

All right, Charlie. As you take on this second round, that's your new chant.

—The Sender

PS: I'm going higher.

CHARLIE DIDN'T KNOW the reality of it when he showed up Monday morning, but he faced a dark and difficult period of chemo. He was going to have to go higher. After that he could go home for another recovery period. But that was some way off in the future with lots of suffering on the road to get there.

A small stack of letters from the Sender awaited him in his room. Charlie read through them all. He took mad notes and even began the process of going back through his shoebox to read all the earlier unopened letters, adding notes in his small spiral notebook. He even marked a couple letters and sent them off to Max in a large manila envelope. Max would love them. The letters were all, as cherry-cheeked braggart Bing noted, really good.

Come to think of it, where was Bing? Charlie hadn't seen him all day and that was a real surprise. No matter, Charlie thought; he'd show up. He always did. Charlie picked up one of the new letters and began reading.

Hey, buddy.

Deion Sanders always used to say, "The play don't care who makes it." I kind of didn't understand what he meant until I suddenly got it. What he was really saying is, you never know when the play is going to occur. You just have to make sure you show up when the play shows up. That's different than forcing it. There's a difference between letting it happen and making it happen.

The Dallas Cowboys had an all-pro wide receiver whose first career catch was a sixty-nine-yard bomb in the third quarter of his first game. Their offensive coordinator taught him a lesson he never forgot: "You never know when the play is going to show. The problem is, if it doesn't show in the first quarter or the second quarter, you quit trying. Then the ball shows up in the third quarter and you are not there."

Hey, Charlie, you never know when health is going to show up, so you always gotta be in position. You have to be there when it does. You never know when a blessing is going to show up. You have to be there when it does. I've always thought financially, economically, you never know when it's going to show up. It can come in so many differently disguised ways.

So a lot of winning is about positioning. A lot of

health is about positioning too. I worked with a guy who is a wholesaler for a financial company. He's very successful. I said, "How are you a success?" He goes, "Everybody who is a financial advisor that does well eats in this deli each morning. So guess where I eat each morning?" It's all about positioning. Forget about your condition: it's about position.

What is the position of health? It's about not forcing it to happen. It's about sitting in a position and letting it come. You might call it prayer. I pray about the problem, pray about the solution. It's about pausing your thoughts. Here you go, Dog, this is it: Living in your vision and not living in your circumstances. That's the position. It's about taking quiet walks with your wife and getting your body in that rhythm. My grandmother used to always sing that song, "I come to the garden alone, when the dew is still on the roses. He walks with me and He talks with me . . ."

I wake up every morning and take that position, Charlie. I look at the ceiling every morning and say, "God has a plan for me." Jeremiah 29:11. God is here, Charlie, and he has a plan for you. Jeremiah 29:11. Just keep saying that over and over every morning lying in bed.

Let me tell you what we are doing with this second

round of chemo. There was a boxer named Cyclone Hart. And he loses this fight to an Italian named Vito. And at the end of the fight they were in the locker room and there was a curtain between them. And this guy Vito started talking to his trainer. Cyclone Hart could hear him. And Vito said, "He kept on hitting me with that left in my ribs. And I thought to myself that if he hits me one more time with that left, I'm going to quit. But he never hit me again. I don't know why, he just quit hitting me."

Cyclone Hart, on the other side of the curtain, started to cry. And he said quietly to his trainer, "I didn't think my left was getting there."

Let me show you what we are doing with this chemo, Charlie. We are hitting cancer in its ribs one more time with our left. People don't realize they have to keep hitting. They don't think their punches are landing. We are going to keep throwing lefts. We are Cyclone Hart and this hard left punch will make Vito quit. That's what this is. You are going into remission soon. Just give him one more shot in the left ribs. Positioning.

There are two things. Stay in position where health comes, Charlie. It's like when I used to work with the Pittsburgh Penguins, they would lose their *mind about Gretzky. They'd say, "Oh, Gretzky's going to be in his office tonight." You know where Gretzky's office was, Charlie? It's that little piece of ice right behind the net. And he would sit back there because he knew that's where the goals would come from. And they would all come down the ice and he would just slip out and go back into his office.*

Stay in Gretzky's office. How? In my mind Gretsky's office really has nothing to do with ice or hockey or anything else. It's about making a choice to keep your mind in the right place. Gretzky's office is prayer, pausing your thinking, staying on the vision, your daughters' weddings, the state championship trophy, time with your wife and family, and things like that. Legend has it that Willie Sutton, the famous bank robber, was asked why he robbed banks, and he said, "Because that's where the money is." Use that, Charlie: stay on the field where the money is. This spot. Where the money is here is prayer, pause of thought and vision. And one last thing, one more shot in the ribs and it goes down. This is a good letter, huh? I'm still fired up from reading the scores of your Bucks. Five in a row, bro. All right, my man. Go punch it in the ribs one more time.

—The Sender

That was good. He reached for his notebook and scribbled a few lines. He'd use this letter again. And he vowed to give this positioning business a good try. Every morning he'd wake up and say, "God has a plan for me."

And he did.

There was another letter in the pile that really clicked for him. The Sender talked about separating the "Who from the Do."

Charlie, it's me.

My little boy Jared tried out for basketball, but he's short like me. When it comes to sports, he plays real hard but he has the wrong parents. I used to get awards all the time for being the hardest-working, most dedicated. But I was thinking, "Why am I on the bench?" It bothered me. Still does.

I love the story where Moses sent a group to look at the land of milk and honey for the Israelites to seize. And they came back with what they called an evil report. "Yes, the land flows with milk and honey, but there are giants up there and we are grasshoppers." The only ones who had no fear were Caleb and Joshua.

Caleb and Joshua were the only ones from that original group to go into the Promised Land because of how they saw themselves: strong and capable. Be Caleb. Be Joshua.

I was in southern California last week and I was told of a study where they tested the Pygmalion effect on some elementary school kids. The Pygmalion effect says that people's performance lines up with what's expected of them. How you label them affects their performance. I was told this story during a break so I can't vouch for its scienctific accuracy, but researchers randomly selected ninety kids and three teachers. They told the three teachers, "These are the best ninety kids in southern California and you are the three best teachers." Those teachers taught those ninety kids for a full year and at the end of the year they had the highest test scores. So the researchers brought the teachers in and said, "We lied. Those aren't the ninety best kids. They were just randomly selected. We lied a second time. You are not the three best teachers." The labels you use on people affect them.

Let me put this in practical terms now. Here goes: you gotta separate the who from the do. When something happens to you, that's the do, not the who. Right now you are going through an illness but that's not who you are. If I'm sick, that doesn't mean that's who

I am. If I am broke, if my marriage fails, I'm not a failure. Separate the who from the do.

One of my favorite plays is Man of LaMancha. *Don Quixote met this prostitute, Aldonza. But he just refused to see her that way. He didn't believe that's what God made her and he started calling her Lady Dulcinea.* Dulce *means "sweet" in Spanish—Don Quixote saw her as sweet. At the end, that's what she became. Separate the who from the do.*

You are not a human being having a spiritual experience, you are a spiritual being having a human experience. You are a spiritual being having an ill experience. I want you to just chant with yourself constantly, "God made me a strong, healthy being. And give me time, I am going to place this right back in the hands of God and say, 'God, just make me what you intended me to be, a healthy, strong man.'" This one was good. I just woke up with this one. Pretty good, huh?

—*The Sender*

Yeah. Pretty good. Charlie found himself moved by these simple, striking ideas. He was moved more by them than just about anything in the last few years. There was something so forceful yet uncomplicated about them. They just made him feel deeply enthused. They were the right message at the right moment. *He wanted to share them.*

That was it! That was the urge that had been plaguing him: he wanted to share. No coaching or yelling or scheming or strategizing, just sharing the message.

Though at times still intemperate and volatile, Charlie was thawing deep inside. For some key people in his life it was not soon enough.

His first thought was Max. Yeah, Max. He scribbled off a note about throwing left punches and put the letter in the mail to Max. Then his mind turned to Bing. He hadn't been around.

Charlie asked a nurse. Bad news: Bing had been moved to a different unit for more intensive treatment. Cancer makes everything worse and being an overweight guy with preexisting health issues is a wicked mix. He was in intensive care and would likely be there for a while.

Charlie paid him a visit.

It was a bad scene. Bing had IVs plugged into his arms and his normally crimson-red face was ashen. He looked swollen and the sparkle in his eyes had vanished. You get used to seeing sick people in a cancer ward, but Bing looked like he was on his final lap.

"What's up, Dog?" Charlie asked as he sidled up beside Bing's bed.

"Who you callin' Dog?" Bing shot back.

"I need to talk to you about some money I won from you in a card game, remember?" Charlie said.

"No chance of that, hustler," Bing said. "Nice try though."

They both chuckled quietly, like you do in a hospital. Charlie just wasn't used to seeing big Bing laid out like this. Bing was always visiting him, sharing his nonsense and boasting about being superman. Seeing him in this condition was awkward, and Charlie had almost no idea what to say.

"I got a coupla new letters here you might be interested in reading," he began. "You look like you could use some good cheer."

"Yeah, Charlie, they say I'm not doing well, and to be honest they're right. I'm just not myself."

Charlie thought it an understatement, but was happy to hear something honest and genuine finally coming out of Bing's mouth.

"These letters will hit the spot. I haven't even read them but I'm sure they're good."

"Can you do me a favor, Charlie? Can you read one to me? I really like those letters but I just don't have the energy to read. Would you mind?"

Charlie was not a reader. He was a coach. But Bing

suddenly just looked like a vulnerable human being in need of the simplest thing. Seeing the big man down, Charlie figured he'd give it a shot. He reached into his gown pocket and retrieved one of the old letters neither one of them had read.

"Will do, Bing. You ready?"

"Do it, Coach," came Bing's exhausted reply.

All right Charlie.

I was a junior in college and I had to write a paper on exercise physiology. I was a biology major and a coaching major. I went to grab a book on exercise physiology and I pulled out a book on sports psychology by accident. I loved it. I read it until about six, seven, or eight that night, I just kept reading it.

I came home. My dad was drinking. We sat down together for dinner. My dad was in no mood for a serious discussion, so we started to eat. My two sisters were out on dates. My mom was working. I said, "Dad, I know what I'm going to do with my life." He said, "What?" I said, "I'm going to be a sports psychologist for the Pittsburgh Steelers, the Dallas Cowboys, and the United States Olympic Committee." My dad never graduated from high school. He said, "What's that? What's a sports psychologist do?" I said, "I don't know."

He just looked at me, and I can still see his eyes, and he says, "Just eat."

Ten years later I finished up my doctorate. I was presenting a paper at West Virginia, and three people were in my group. All three walked out when I was done. They didn't say anything to me. Eight months later I walked into my office in West Virginia and the secretary said, "You just got an invitation to go work with the United States Olympic Committee. Call this number if you are interested." I said, "What?" She said, "Yes, when you presented that paper in April, one of the men was from the Olympic Committee. He's the vice president. There's only three of them. He wants you to work for him."

While I'm there at the Olympic Committee, the guy I coached high school football with—his name was Tommy—left high school and went to coach at a junior college, and then went to the Steelers. Now he's the GM of the Steelers. He calls me to work for the Steelers because they keep messing up on draft picks. Missing them on attitude. He wants me to develop a scouting system for attitude and now I'm with them. While I was with the Steelers, we played the Dallas Cowboys in the Super Bowl. We beat them up but our quarterback threw two interceptions and they beat us *on the scoreboard. But we really manhandled them. Jerry Jones came to the ownership of the Steelers and said, "What's going on with you guys? I spent a lot more money than you did and you shouldn't have done that to us." And my name came up and Jerry hired me. Isn't that kind of weird? Kind of like a booga booga."*

Bing chuckled. *Booga booga.*

Viktor Frankl called it "dereflection." Today we would call it visualization. When he was in the Nazi concentration camps it was very uncomfortable. He would set for himself a mental stage and make an image in his mind where he was standing at a podium in a large lecture hall. He was lecturing about a theory he developed while he was in the camps called Logotherapy. He later wrote about it in his book Man's Search for Meaning. *And when he got out of the concentration camp, he spent the rest of his life lecturing people about his ideas.*

There's just something about seeing something and then having it happen.

I'll give you another example. I was working with the New Orleans Saints and they had a rookie who was going to be the next big thing. He wanted to work with me, but all the veterans were getting on him. "You can't work him! You are too big time." But he wanted to be great. He was open to anything. So he came to me and sat down and visualized that he would come across the quarterback, smack the ball loose, scoop it up, and run for the touchdown.

They had a game that week and wouldn't you know it: he comes around, smacks the quarterback, ball comes loose, he runs for a touchdown. I don't know if God played a trick on somebody. It doesn't work just like that, right? I came back into New Orleans the next time and as soon as I came to the door, he was standing right inside the door with his notebook. He thought I was Houdini or something.

A man named Captain Jack Sands was shot down and went into the Hanoi Hilton in Vietnam as a prisoner. Every day for seven years he visualized playing the golf course where he grew up. He was never able to break 90 on that course. When he got out, he went to Bethesda for rehab. When he was done, he went home and golfed that course he'd been visualizing hundreds of times. He shot 74, two over par.

I want you to spend time each day visualizing. I want you to have four different scripts. Write them out thoroughly. Like a dream. Coaching on the sideline.

Healthy as can be. Running up and down the sideline. Hugging your ball players. Screaming at a ref because he made a bad call. Thrilled with what's going on. High-fiving guys. Squeaking out the victory.

I want you to write out another script. You and Eve in Florence, Italy. No kids. You and Eve in Naples. Drinking good wine. Healthy as can be. Just having a blast.

Let's do a third script. I want you to see yourself walking down the aisle with your daughter. She's in a beautiful gown getting married. Emotional. Eve waiting down there for you. "Who gives this young lady?" Feel that emotion. Then I want you to see yourself dancing at the reception.

Let's do this last dereflection. I want you to see yourself winning the state high school championship. Getting that trophy. Hoisting it. Just screaming out to the crowd and the television cameras. Maybe yelling my name: "This one's for you, friend! This one's for you!" Yeah, baby.

Charlie, there's something to this. There's been a lot of cancer research that says this visualization, dereflection stuff isn't the whole ball of wax. But there's something to it. And I want you to dereflect everyday.

You've got time on your hands. The uncomfortableness you have right there inside you, go somewhere else. Use your eyes; see yourself as healthy. See yourself at the state championship and don't you forget hoisting that big trophy, Dog.

—The Sender

"Dog," Bing said with a tired, wheezing chuckle.

"Four scripts," Charlie repeated, almost to himself.

"What are th . . . again?" Bing puffed.

"Uh, let me see . . . One, running up and down the sideline, excited and high-fiving your players; two, having fun with your wife; three, walking down the aisle with your daughter; and four, winning the state championship. He says here to write them out and visualize them."

"Don't feel like writing . . ." Bing whispered.

"Then just see them. See them real good," Charlie said.

He had a sudden thought that it wasn't that long ago that he was the one needing the coaching. And now here he was, not feeling all that great himself but giving a shot in the heart to someone who needed it. It was a strange feeling but a good one.

Then, lost in his thoughts, he noticed in a flash that while he was reading that letter he was . . . dereflecting. He was so lost in something, something so real on the stage in his mind that his pain and discomfort were gone. That had to be a good thing . . . and if nothing else the relief was wonderful.

Maybe there *was* something to all this.

Charlie looked at Bing lying in his bed. He was fast asleep now. Dreaming, Charlie hoped, of walking his daughter down the aisle.

He slipped the other letter under Bing's pillow, and quietly crept out of the room.

CHAPTER .16

THE WEEK CRAWLED BY and the chemo was making Charlie sicker by the hour. By Friday he could barely lift himself up off the bed and felt the worst nausea and fatigue of his life. But that was the night of another big game. He knew he had to rally to listen to the game, but he had so little energy. Yet he stirred when his daily letter showed up. This afternoon the tattooed woman delivered it. He never did get her name. His mind was just closed to tattoos and anyone who had them. He didn't want to know her. "Just a leeeetle steeck," she'd say, her voice drawn out and sing-songy, right before she'd nail him.

Today she didn't look so good. Her face was sallow and she seemed distracted. She said little. She just sort of stared and shuffled around listlessly. Then she reached in her lab-coat pocket and pulled out a letter, laying it on his bedside tray. For reasons he cannot say his mind cleared suddenly as he watched her. Suddenly he didn't think of the pain, just her.

"Dulcinea," he said out of nowhere.

"Huh?" she replied, turning her head and focusing on him.

"What's your name?" he asked. "I never did know."

"Leah," she replied. "Thank you for asking."

"Do you mind if I call you Dulcinea?" he asked, thinking back on what he'd read in one of the letters still lying on the tray.

"Who is Dulcinea?"

Charlie smiled.

"You look bothered by something," he replied. "You reminded me of this letter I got. You know I've been getting a lot of these. I found one I thought you might like to read."

"That's nice," she replied blankly.

"Really. Do you want to see it? It's about things you'll like. Especially if you feel bad."

Cancer, it seemed, was making Charlie a better listener. But he was tiring quickly. Just that short conversation wiped him out.

"I feel blue, honey, I'll tell you that," Leah drawled, her sing-song tone gone.

In his exhaustion and for only a moment, Charlie saw her. No tattoos, no bad breath, no needles, no "*leetle steeck*." Just her. No condescension or judgment; just one hurting person looking at another.

Charlie motioned to the opened letter sitting on the tray. The "Who from the Do" letter.

"Dulcinea," he whispered. "It's all in the note. Please take it and read."

Leah picked up the letter and looked at it. She'd never been offered anything by a patient before. She read the first few lines.

"Thank you, Charlie. I need this. I will read it—"

She looked back down at Charlie. He was already out.

CHAPTER .17

CHARLIE AWOKE LATE that night, well after dark, refreshed but still hurting. Moving through chemo round number two: that was a bright spot. He rolled slightly to reach a small tube set up to help him drink water. He sipped and savored. "Water," he mused. Simple. Wonderful.

He turned over and flipped on the radio next to his bed. He saw that he was late for the game but he wanted to catch any bit of it that he could. The game was over and the announcers were wrapping up their coverage. The Bucks won a close one over the Homewood Patriots, a team they should've beaten badly. He'd find out what happened, but nevertheless was happy for the victory. The Bucks were 6–2 and rolling along.

It was unusually quiet on the floor that evening. He turned off the radio and felt a strange and sudden jolt of energy, so he sat himself up as best he could. He looked at his spindly arms. They were emaciated and pale. His bones hurt. He was a shrinking heap of skin and bones and pain. Out of habit his mind drifted to his still sadly deep and hopeless dilemma. He knew that's how deep depression begins for cancer patients. Then suddenly he stopped his racing mind. With some intention and direction he just made his mind stop racing off. He felt strangely strong and capable on the inside.

He'd never noticed the difference between the inside and the outside so much. It was probably always there; he just didn't notice. Maybe it was because all his life his body was so strong. His attention was so much on external strength. There was no need for inner strength. But now that his body was nearly gone the difference between inner and outer was easy to see. He didn't think about these things much before, but he did now.

He reached for the new letter Leah brought earlier, sitting on his tray. This letter looked familiar but it was not from the Sender. This one was from Max! Charlie was overjoyed; the sort of joy that comes when you connect with another human and they love something as much as you. Max was answering some long unsolved mystery deep inside the heart of Coach Cristo.

The envelope had something in it. He opened it quickly and smiled with delight at what he saw: three Popsicle sticks. No note, just three old Popsicle sticks with red stains halfway up. One of them was signed by Max and the other two by a couple of Charlie's players who had visited Max in the hospital.

Charlie was slightly blown away by that. His boys visiting one another all on their own. Something he'd said or done worked. It touched him how a small gesture can radiate from person to person so fast.

"Perfect," Charlie murmured, "just perfect. Stick around, stick around, stick around, you wonderful young dogs!" Charlie chuckled.

He set the small wooden sticks down and decided to send Max another letter. He looked through his growing spiral notebook of letter notes to find some ideas of what to say to Max. He was really starting to rely on those quick jots. He knew why: for the first time in his life he had something fresh to say. Something to share in those void moments when you want to say something powerful but haven't any words, much less the right ones. It seemed to him that the reason people didn't like talking to sick people is that it was just too real: nobody had anything they considered worthy of the magnitude of the moment and were afraid of saying the wrong thing. And all the sick person wanted was for someone to show up. Now, Charlie could show up with powerful words. He didn't remember ever feeling so valuable.

As he thumbed through his notebook he came across something perfect. It was a note he'd received from the Sender early in his stay. He had them fairly well cross-referenced by now and was able to quickly put his hand on the actual note in the box. It was perfect: a great story about a twelve-year-old with cancer.

Charlie, it's me.

I'm in Charlotte, North Carolina, right now. And there was a man who came up to me. He was a financial advisor. And his daughter's name was Summer. And she had cancer real bad. She was a little girl. She didn't have the diagnosis you have and she wasn't going to make it. She knew it.

So you know what she did? She went to Make-A-Wish of Charlotte and she said, "I know what I want to do." The dad didn't know what she was going to ask for. She said, "Here's my wish: my wish is that you allow me to grant wishes." They said, "What?" "My wish is that you allow me to grant wishes." They had never heard anything like that before. "That's what I want."

That little girl spent the rest of her life granting wishes. How do you think the rest of her life went?

I got an idea. I want you to keep getting better

because I want me and you to grant wishes. I want to go out. I want to go be with you. I want us to win and I want us to spend all of our life like Summer, granting wishes. That's the lesson tonight for your spirit. Go grant wishes.

You are going to know pain and discomfort and the other side of struggle like few have. Let's go grant wishes. I want you to keep getting better. And every morning as you are getting up saying, "There's a plan for me," I want you to add something to it. "I know what the plan is. You want me to go grant wishes."

Remember that song that was out when we were kids? "What the world needs now, is love, sweet love . . ." Remember that one? I know what the world needs right now. I know exactly what the world needs right now. The world needs you.

—*The Sender*

Charlie nearly choked up reading that one. After thinking carefully about the message for a moment, Charlie rewrote the story slightly in his own hand, folded it up neatly, addressed the letter to Max and forwarded it on.

Then he had momentary flash of irrational fear: *What if Max—?* It was an unthinkably dark shadow of a possibility that felt horrible. He shoved it from his mind and imagined Max taking this letter literally and doing what few adults do: acting on it. Max would be granting someone's wish shortly after reading this note. And many lives would benefit greatly from him.

CHAPTER .18

A DAY OR THREE PASSED—Charlie wasn't really keeping count—and he had to face that fact that he was developing a taxing reputation related to sharing his letters from the Sender: *He* was becoming a magnet for people who needed encouragement. An unmistakable wave of sick and hurting people were moving in his direction. Just showing up. They seemed to come from all over the hospital. This he could not have predicted and did not want. People—the hungry, heartsick, empty, and hopeless—were just coming out of nowhere. He didn't have the energy for any of it.

He got a fast reply from his little buddy Max and it lifted his spirits just in time. Though Charlie was so tired and had such a hard time focusing, Max's innocent crayon scribbles told a different story. He was making dreams come true. He said everyone on the floor loved music, so he made their dreams come true by learning and singing their favorite songs for them. He drew some really bad, really lovable pictures of it.

Charlie just lifted his head toward the ceiling and smiled.

"That's my boy." Sickness has an antidote and Charlie was learning that it just might include love.

This round of chemo was rough and most days he just didn't have the energy to respond to anyone the way he was learning to, wanted to, or knew that he could. He didn't have the cure for cancer, but he had the growing reputation for curing the fear and uncertainty that surrounded it.

Where would the energy come from to help? He needed to pass along the cure no matter how much energy it required, but he had none. Somehow he had to rally and help these people, he just didn't know how.

Then he got a letter that taught him where to find more energy.

Hi, Charlie.
I'm out here on the soccer field watching my boy and I thought of something. I'm going to let all the doctors and the nurses and all the professionals take care of your body and your cancer, but I want to talk to you about your eyes. Think about the car you drive right

now. The day after you bought that car, did you not see that car everywhere? I bought a BMW. I didn't know there were seven hundred BMWs on my block. I put a CB radio in mine though to make me different. What did they do, ship those cars in?

What happened is, at the back of your brain, the back of your head, there's something called the reticular activation system. You will see twenty-five thousand things today. Maybe not so many, since you are sitting in a hospital, but you will see a lot. You won't remember seeing most of them.

After you bought that car your reticular activation system changed. Now you start seeing your car everywhere. It's the eyes. I want to talk to you about conditioning your eyes.

When I spoke to the Packers the first time, I almost got beat up. I mentioned teeny-tiny Appalachian State beating the mighty Michigan in football. The Packers had a Heisman Trophy winner from Michigan. He jumped up and said, "I don't like that story, boy." I can only bench press a hoagie so that was an issue.

The quarterback of Appalachian State was interviewed after the game. He said that they beat the favored Wolverines by watching them on film over and over and over until they saw opportunity. They focused all their energy on watching for opportunity. When they walked in there that day, they weren't looking for Michigan, they were looking for opportunity. And they saw it.

I want you to start saying it and praying it. Here it comes. Ready? "I'm not looking for blessings to come into my life. I'm looking to be a blessing in someone's life."

Charlie scribbled that one in his notebook.

Did you catch that? Read it again. Read it again because when you get it, it will change your eyes. It will change what you see. It will shift your energy.

I was walking through an airport in Tampa about a year ago. "Can I be a blessing in someone's life?" I was saying to myself. There was a woman standing at the Southwest counter, screaming. I walked up to her and I said, "I think I'm looking for you." She said, "The police just came to my door two hours ago and told me my daughter was blown up in a Humvee in Afghanistan. Both of her femurs are broken. All of her ribs are broken. Eighty-five percent of her body is burnt and they medevacked her from Afghanistan to Carmel, Indiana, St. Vincent Hospital. I told the police to take me to the airport. I didn't even lock my house up." I asked her, "Where's your luggage?" She said "I don't have any. I don't need any." "How long are you staying?" I asked. She said, "Months if I have to." "Don't you have anything?" I asked. She said, "A driver's license."

I said, "Well, you don't need anything, you've got me."

Now I go by people every day and never see that kind of need. Why? Because I focus on me, that's why. How come I never saw her before? Because I sit and focus on what's wrong, and I sit and complain and all I see are things to complain about.

We need to redirect our minds to see the things we want to see. So when I walk about saying, "Can I be a blessing, can I be a blessing?" I begin seeing a chance to be a blessing.

And it gives you big jolts of energy to be a blessing, to feel like you are needed, necessary.

Go be necessary to someone. I want you to just go and be a blessing. The next time you have any days like you had the last couple, just pray, "Can I be a

*blessing?" And when you see some chance that you can,
just say something kind to everyone because you can.
Without even trying, you are a blessing. Go be a blessing. Go be necessary to somebody.*

—The Sender

Charlie put the letter down and thought long and hard
about the words. It was so simple: be a blessing. Actually,
just the thought of being a blessing like that to someone
gave him a short burst of energy. He pulled out his notebook and reread his important ideas. "Be a blessing" was
the last entry. He was sure he'd revisit that lesson again
and again.

He was about to add a new one to his growing list, one
he'd read weeks ago. *Lessons get tested.*

It took only moments. As he sat in bed scribbling in his
notebook he heard a commotion in the normally hushed
hallway. A young orderly carrying a food tray had acciden-
tally bounded around a corner and rammed a young female
patient in a wheelchair. The tray went one way, the orderly
another, and the young woman sat crying in the middle in
her wheelchair, her head covered in applesauce.

The woman was inconsolable. She wept and wept in
that unmistakable "last straw" kind of misery.

Her name was Pearly. She was the mother of two young boys. She'd been diagnosed with the most aggressive form of breast cancer and was undergoing a hazardous treatment protocol following a double mastectomy. It was not going well, and she'd spent the morning wrestling with even more bad news from her doctors. She trembled under the load of her unstoppable fate. Her feeble little body quivered uncontrollably and the accident in the hallway pushed her beyond her crumbly limit. She sobbed and sobbed. The dam had broken. It had nothing to do with applesauce.

Charlie gathered himself, rose from the bed, and, though dog tired, made his way to the doorway. There he saw this woman, a fragile, young human being, a person he'd seen nearly every day but never really noticed, utterly dissolve less than ten feet from his door. Though surrounded by helpful staff and nurses trying their best to make the situation right, she was alone at the bottom of life. She was nearing the end of her game and she knew it. She continued to weep lost and lonely tears, forlorn and without any discernible hope, utterly broken. It shattered Charlie's heart. The relentless cruelty of this disease seemed to eventually break the will of everyone it touched.

Charlie stepped out into the hallway to help, but was urged by the staff to stay in his room. He watched the nurses and orderlies clean up the mess. He just stared at the young mother as she was wheeled back to her room down the hall.

In that instant Charlie shifted on the inside. *Haphak* is the name for moments like that. Charlie read it in one of the earlier letters. It's an Old Testament Hebrew word for a *turning-point moment*. A turnaround, when an *implosion* turns into an *explosion*. For Charlie this *haphak* felt like a moment of pure, honest clarity; a sudden and unexpectedly clear sense of fate. It was a bold and dramatic calling. He felt suddenly steeled on the inside; filled with determination and purpose his cancer had hijacked long ago. With this steel he would build a life committed to showing people how to win the game of living. In that moment he became something new.

CHAPTER .19

THE NEXT DAY CHARLIE DECIDED to share the *haphak* idea with Max and hoped that he'd understand. It was a lot like teaching football players something new and unexpected. In this case, Hebrew. And Charlie wouldn't be around to coach it. He'd just have to send it out and see what connected.

He jotted a quick note to Max. He coached him to turn his life into a great explosion of love. That's all Charlie could think to say. "Just love people more and more, young blood. Bring it! *Haphak*!" he wrote.

When he was done he dropped his pen, sealed the envelope, and set it out for someone to drop in the mail. He lay his head back and began thinking. Though he was so tired, he began thinking about the Sender and all these crazy letters. He began thinking about how these words had been the right messages at the right time for him. And they'd changed him.

He couldn't help but wonder what to do with all this.

Coaches get good at figuring out what the opponent is trying to do. It's part of the job. Charlie spent a lot of time that day trying to figure out the game plan of the Sender. Then came the letter that clarified everything.

I'm going to teach you a principle right here and when I learned it, it changed my life. Here it comes, Coach . . . get ready . . . this is it . . . take notes: When you go after something like cancer, marriage, or your job you've got to hit it on three different levels all at once. This very short story explains all three pieces.

In Exodus 17:9–13, Moses needed to fight a great battle. He instructed Joshua to go down into the valley to fight the Amalekites, while he, Moses, went high up on a rock and held up the staff of God. And when his arms were up, the Israelites won, and when his arms dropped the Israelites lost. So when his arms got tired, Aaron and Hur came up on the rock and lifted Moses's hands up. And the Israelites won the battle.

That's the whole thing, Dog!

So let's go over this again. You have to win on three dimensions or levels:

Dimension #1: Spiritual. You have to win the spiritual plane. The lifting of the arms is the lifting of the spirit. Through prayer. Through pause of thought.

Through focusing on what you want to achieve and believing.

Dimension #2: Physical. You have to win on the physical plane. The fighting down in the valley with the sword is doing the process. Doing the right things. Doing the work. Focusing not on the battle, but on doing the work of winning the battle.

Dimension #3: Relational. You have to win the relational plane. The lifting of the arms of one another is what to do when you get tired. We need people around us to lift us. I hope and pray that was one of the things I've done for you in your life. Lifting your arms when you couldn't lift them yourself.

Let me explain all this.

First, lifting the spirit. I've got a friend in Pittsburgh who told me, "I hate my boss." He had a job making about $250,000 a year. I said, "You are going to get fired." He said, "No, I'm doing all the work. I'm presenting. I'm closing." (He was in sales.) I said, "You don't get it. You are fighting down in a valley with a sword but you are not up on the rock lifting your arms. You need to lift your spirits first, so you can stay focused on what you really want."

So I taught this story to Green Bay going into the playoffs of their Super Bowl year. Our quarterback missed a pass against Atlanta. But if you go watch the film, it was a classic example: he and the head coach looked at each other and they lifted their arms. And went on to win the game. In other words, the first thing you do is lift the spirit.

Second, do the work. I had heard so many stories and I've seen this a couple of times where people have gotten sick and they were of a religion that they weren't allowed to treat it. In other words, they are taught to lift their spirits through prayer alone. But they don't do the work. They don't do the practical. They don't do the physical.

I see these people all the time. Their heads are in the clouds. They are walking around praying about everything. But they don't do the work. And I know the other too. I know people who do the work constantly but they never lift their spirits.

You need to do them both.

Let's get to the last one, lifting arms. When Moses's arms were tired out, Aaron and Hur got on each side of him and lifted them. A good friend of mine got fired as the head coach at a major university, and you know what he called and told me? He said, "I did this to me. I didn't think I needed anybody. I didn't call you." In other words, he didn't get anybody around him to lift his arms.

I'm going to suggest that you need to win on all three different dimensions at once. You are lifting the spirit when you say, "I will beat this." You are doing the physical when you are getting treated and you are getting the chemo. You said you were down and lifting weights. Good luck with that. But you are doing the physical. That's what the doctors were trying to teach you when one day they said, "Charlie, you can't let this thing beat you psychologically." And you beat it on the third level when you let people love you and lift you up when you can't do it yourself.

There was a woman I was talking to in Louisiana. And she had advanced breast cancer and the doctor told her she was going to be fine. She said, "You told another woman she wasn't going to be fine and hers isn't as bad as mine." He said, "Yes, but she shut out her family." She didn't have anybody to lift her arms.

I'm not sure why God does what he does. I'm not smart enough. I love what my daughter Claire did one day to my boy Jared. She was trying to explain something. Jared said he didn't understand something about God, about why things go this way. And my little Claire walked Jared over to our dog, Ellabelle, and said "Jared, do you know how Ella, compared to us—she doesn't understand some things that we understand?" Jared said, "Yes." Claire said, "Well, compared to God, me and you have a doggie mind." Whew.

I don't know why God does things that he does. There's a hurricane going on right now as I write to you. I was in Tuscaloosa right after the tornadoes destroyed it several years ago. To be honest with you, I don't get it. But I wonder if God wants to give us opportunities to hold up other people's arms.

Charlie, give everybody the opportunity to keep holding up your arms. I think I've got a doggie mind here, but trying to play God. But if there is a reason why these things happen: it's a setup so that we can walk in and hold up one another's arms.

Fight this thing on three levels. Keep doing the treatment. Keep doing the diet. Keep doing the exercise. Keep doing the prayer. Keep doing the pause for affirmations. Keep going to bed and saying, "God has a plan for me." And I want you today to tell someone, "Come on in here and lift up my arms." Give them an opportunity to love you. Winning on three fronts. And after you beat this, we are going to go win the state championship on three dimensions.

—The Sender

Lesson learned.

LESSONS GET TESTED.

A few of Charlie's players came to see him early Sunday morning. They'd won their Friday-night game against the Vestavia Rebels and now stood on the edge of greatness at 7–2. They kept thanking Charlie over and over for his pep talks and letters. The team was steamrolling now. If they won the upcoming Friday-night game against Mountain Brook they'd make the playoffs. The Bucks were back.

As the boys left Charlie handed them a letter that he was sure would help them. Charlie called it the "Friday Night Lights OUT!" letter. He asked if any of the captains could read. That drew a laugh, and Andrew, the quarterback, quickly volunteered to take the reading duties on the coming Friday night.

We're gonna make it to the playoffs tonight. How big is your circle?

114

In the first century BC, Israel was going through a drought. And belief was at a low level. For four centuries there hadn't been any prophets; for four centuries, no one had really believed they'd heard from God. The drought was literally threatening their extinction as a people.

And the history books recorded that there was a man named Honi. And he was famous for his ability to pray for rain. And he believed that even though nobody had heard from God, God could hear from him.

So the people gathered around one day outside the walls of Jerusalem, and Honi walked outside the walls with a six-foot staff in his hands. And the history books said he took the staff and drew a circle. 90, 180, 270, 360 degrees. Then in the middle of the circle, he dropped to his knees and he raised his hands to heaven. He said, "Lord of the universe. Your great name. I will not move from this circle until you show mercy on your children."

What moved them was the authority with which he spoke. Then it happened. History recorded that a light drizzle started. And everyone started looking up at the skies but Honi didn't. How big is your circle?

Honi said, "I'm not praying for rain, Lord. I'm praying that all the cisterns, all the pits, all the caves, all the caverns, are filled with water from your down-pour." It came harder. He still didn't move from his circle. He goes, "I'm not praying for rain, God. I'm praying for favor on your children. I'm praying for blessings. I'm praying for your graciousness." And the rains and the heavens opened up and he got a downpour.

Of course, many judged him. The Sanhedrin judged him and brought him in and tried to excommunicate him, but people don't understand that good always wins. Not initially, but eventually. And the people said, "No. No. Don't condemn him! Not for what he did." Keep this in mind when people criticize you. They've never erected a statue to a critic.

If somebody is doing something great, like you guys, keep one thing in mind about Honi's prayer. He wasn't saying, "Benefit me." This is different. He was praying for all God's children. He wanted well-being for all.

What are you praying for the Seminole Valley Bucks? Okay, you've got a great team. But now, why don't you start praying for the caves to be full. Is your circle big enough? Pray for all the cisterns to be over-flowing. Why don't you even pray for favor? Not for you, for all the Bucks everywhere around town! Inspire *people. Make your circle bigger. You are my boys! You've done wonderful things. Big prayers have been answered. Bigger circle. Bigger prayer. Next step. The Bible says you have not because you ask not. Bigger circle, Honi. Bigger circle. Ask for a BIG STORM tonight, Honi!*

—*The Sender*

The boys thanked him, each hugged him tightly and they left the room. The group of them passed Pearly sitting quietly in her wheelchair in the hallway. They didn't notice her, or perhaps in their discomfort they just avoided eye contact and kept walking.

But Charlie saw her.

HE'D NOT SEEN PEARLY since the applesauce incident. She sat sullenly in her wheelchair, covered with a blanket and watching people pass with her eyes, her head lying languidly to the side. She kept to herself, probably not feeling very chatty.

Charlie had talked to her husband a day or two earlier and heard the grim news. She was regressing: Stage three triple negative breast cancer. As bad as it gets. In truth, the chances of survival had all but vanished. Doctors had just told her she might need as many as *seventeen rounds of chemo* with a new experimental drug to even have a chance of surviving. The news couldn't be much worse, and Pearly was naturally devastated. Her family had no idea what to tell her.

Charlie asked Pearly's husband if he'd mind him sharing some of his letters with her. The husband, reeling with grief and afraid himself, thanked Charlie over and over for his courage and thoughtfulness.

It was time to put his lessons to work and do some arm lifting. Charlie approached Pearly quietly in the hallway and asked if he might have a seat. Her eyes brightened as she tentatively nodded, certainly wondering why Charlie would have any time for her. He never seemed to before.

Pearly, as her husband had described, was a withdrawn and deeply beaten woman. Pearly was a nurse, newly married, with two boys, one from a previous marriage. She was happy before her diagnosis . . . life was on track for her and her new family and things were going well. Then this.

"I hear you have two boys, Pearly. What are their names?"

"Scotty and Trent," she said, clearing her throat and sitting up slightly with motherly pride. She couldn't have been more than twenty-five or twenty-six years old.

Charlie had the sudden urge to cry. He swallowed hard and it passed.

"How old are they? I have two girls myself. Teenagers."

"Scotty is five and Trent is nine months. They are big, happy boys. I saw your girls. They are very pretty. So is your wife."

Charlie smiled. Fatherly pride.

"I would love to see your boys if they come to visit. I could use some big ones on my team."

"I know you're the coach. My husband played football but he doesn't want our sons getting their heads kicked in."

Charlie smiled.

"It's a common worry, Pearly, and I can't say I blame him. I try to take care of my kids. Most of them have no future in the game so it makes sense to keep it just a game and help them leave with brains full of great memories, not bruises."

Pearly carried on about her boys without further prompting. She was pouring like a broken dam, bursting under the pressure of maternal love, just waiting to open on someone who would simply take the time to listen. She was one with Scotty and Trent as only a mother can be.

The bitterness of the whole deal suddenly caught in Charlie's throat again as he listened. He was honestly thinking about his own girls and how much he loved them.

He swallowed hard, and they continued their talk for many minutes. When Pearly looked as though she might be wearing down, Charlie made his move.

"Pearly, I have been very fortunate over the last couple of months of chemo. I have a friend, I'm not exactly sure who, and he has sent me a letter every single day I've been here."

Pearly raised her eyebrows, listening, saying nothing.

"There is one that came that for whatever reason reminded me of you. I have it here, and if you'd like, you can have it. It might raise your spirits and help keep you focused at a time when you could use it. Would you like it?"

Charlie reached into his robe pocket and retrieved the letter, still in its envelope.

Pearly moved her hand out slowly from beneath her blanket and stretched meekly toward the letter. Her hand was pale and withered, like an icy claw. She trembled slightly. Charlie met her halfway.

"Thank you, Charlie," she said, now barely above a whisper.

"If you want to talk about it, I'd be honored, Pearly. I hope it touches you as it touched me."

Charlie's hand drifted toward hers. He made contact, skin to skin. She felt cold. The color of her hands was very different from his. Charlie kept touching her without moving, quite possibly the only real human connection she'd had in days, besides professionals and her family.

Her eyes rose and tracked him as he stood and retreated to his room. He turned slightly as he walked through his door and watched her slowly opening the letter. She was about to get her arms lifted.

Charlie, I understand your condition. I think I got it pretty well. You've got cancer. You are married to a wonderful woman. You have two beautiful children. That's your condition. But I don't want to talk to you about your condition. I'm not even sure that's a big issue. It's your position I want to talk to you about.

My father was a Marine. He didn't cry a lot. One morning I heard him crying and I came out. "What's wrong?" I asked. He said his mother, my grandmother, had been diagnosed with a rare form of leukemia. This was twenty-five years ago. "She'll be dead in five days," he told me.

So I went down to see her on my bicycle. She was playing an organ and singing songs and I said, "Grandma, Dad said you will be dead in five days." She said, "Who told him that?" I said, "The doctors." She said, "They are not God. I'll go when I'm ready. I need to pray for my kids. I have things to do. I am going to pray for your father first."

Let me explain this to you. Her condition was she had leukemia. Her position was, "I'll go when I'm ready." She died in my senior year of college, many years later. She overcame her condition by her position, by her attitude, what she chose to believe in.

You have to keep on telling yourself something

over and over until you finally believe it. You have to keep believing in spite of the evidence, then watch the evidence change. I like to say fake it until you make it. Your condition is you've got cancer. Your position is you are going to dance at your kids' weddings. Your condition is what the doctors told you it is. That doesn't even mean anything. Your position is they can't do life without you. Your position is this is what will happen.

Every single person who ever beat cancer in their life was not shocked that they beat it. They knew they were going to beat it. They lived in this moment, in this position, not their condition. All right, Charlie, my friend, you keep paying attention to your position and don't you worry about your condition."

—The Sender

About an hour later Charlie came out of his room. He peered down the hall. Pearly was gone.

THE BOYS BEAT THE SPARTANS of Mountain Brook. They were into the state championship cycle and were, for the first time in years, serious contenders. But a lot of football was yet to be played. They had to win three games, culminating in the championship game. Normally the state championship game was played in the Jordan-Hare Stadium on the campus of Auburn University, but this year the venue had been shifted to the hallowed field at Bryant-Denny Stadium at the University of Alabama in Tuscaloosa. For Alabama kids it was like playing a game on the fifty-yard line of heaven. This venue shift created a sense of urgency and excitement among the teams that nobody had ever experienced before.

Charlie was going to be able to make the first play-off game, but would be an inpatient for the next two. If the Bucks won he'd be present for the state championship game. It felt like a fast-moving dream for Charlie.

CHARLIE'S SECOND ROUND of chemo had been the worst by far, yet in some ways the best. The doctors told him he was making great progress and that he should feel good about his progress. All he felt most of the time was putrid and exhausted. Yet he kept . . . *growing*. *Getting better, not bitter*. The letters were finding their mark and he felt more centered, clear, and certain of things than ever before.

If making a difference in other people's lives makes you feel buoyant, Charlie was swimming.

As he packed up to go home for the week, Leah/ Dulcinea, poked her head in the door. She had a letter in her hand. This one from Max.

"Hello, Mr. Quixote," she said playfully.

Charlie, standing with his back to her, chuckled.

"I'm afraid you can't poke me today, my *leetle* friend," he chided, turning around to look at her.

"No sticks today," she said. "You're doing much better

125

and now you get to go home. I just wanted to say thank you for that letter. It didn't cure everything but it made me think."

Charlie smiled again. "Sometimes just thinking something new is a good place to start."

He reached his hand out with another letter for her.

"This will help you on your journey. Read it and know that it comes from my heart."

Charlie was suddenly struck by the fact that he actually had something arm lifting to share with this person. It felt strange. It felt great.

"Thanks, Charlie. You be good and hurry back to see us," she said, placing the letter in her pocket.

"I will, Leah, I will," he replied.

Just then there was a gentle knocking at the door behind Leah. It was Eve. Charlie introduced her to Leah.

"Dulcinea, this is my wife, Eve. Eve, Dulcinea."

Leah blushed, and Eve lunged to hug her. Eve seemed to be hugging everyone these days.

"Such a pretty name! Thank you for all you've all done for Charlie," she said. "I think the old man's gonna be OK."

"Oh, honey, Charlie was born OK," Leah said. "We all love him and want him to get better so bad. I think he's on his way. One more round and he's good as new."

Eve became still at those words, then started tearing up.

Slowly at first. Then a full-on muffled cry. Trying to stop it was pointless. Her emotions were unstoppable.

Charlie stared at her. He'd just had no idea.

Leah excused herself.

Eve's moment was a happy relief cry, filled with genuine affection and gratitude. They'd been through so much.

To break up the moment, Charlie reached for Max's letter. He opened it with a flourish and unfolded a crayon drawing of a boy in a hospital bed sneezing. The caption was simple: *Haphak!* Charlie burst out laughing, between getting the humor and marveling at it. Eve just looked at him in puzzlement.

"I'll explain, when I can," Charlie told her.

The atmosphere in the car on the ride home was practically euphoric. Eve was a changed person. Everything was improving. She told him of the special dinner she'd made and that he and girls were going to have a great evening together as a family. Charlie suddenly remembered his goal for the night and felt in his pocket to be sure he had the letters he wanted to share with his girls. This would be fun.

At about that time Leah/Dulcinea was leaving work at the hospital. She hurried to her car, got in and closed the door and locked it quickly. She never wanted to share her problems with anyone, but she feared for her life at times.

Her jealous ex, the court orders, and a constant state of fear consumed her. She needed a hit of encouragement in more ways than she could ever tell anyone. She had wanted to leave this horrible relationship so many times, but she kept giving in. She quickly reached into her pocket and pulled out the crumpled-up letter Charlie had given her, hoping for something she couldn't even name.

Hi Coach.

When I'm on the road by myself I have long conversations with myself. Most of the time I'm pretty good company for myself. I'll often read something—often it's scripture—and I just kind of contemplate it. The last couple of days it's been John 4:35. "Say not ye, there are yet four months, and then cometh harvest?" Christ was talking to them about procrastination.

There was a guy name W. Clement Stone, who ran a really successful insurance company in Chicago. And he would get his top people together and they would chant over and over and over before they started the day, "Do it now! Do it now! Do it now!" They had great success. Most people don't do it now.

We used to call a certain kind of people when I was growing up "fixin' tos," as in, "I'm fixin' to lose weight." I was trying to explain this to somebody I was counseling. I didn't learn this in my psychology journals. She had a boyfriend for, like, twenty-five years. And she kept on telling me how he loved her and they were fixin' to get married. I guess I hurt her feelings but I told her the truth. I said you are engaged to a fixin' to. He's not going to marry you. She cried. Then she came back a little bit later. She said, "You are right. I just needed somebody to tell me the truth. He's just fixin' to."

Fixin' to. So many times we are fixin' tos. Was there something you ever really wanted to do? Maybe you've already done this, but take Eve to Italy, to Rome. Don't be fixin' to. How about a cruise? Fixin' to. How about calling somebody up and telling them that you love them?

I guess I thought about this with you because, when I went over to study at the International Olympic Academy in Greece, I met a woman whose father was a cancer specialist. While we were over there the PLO was doing some terrorism in the international waters, and my parents were kind of upset. I was about thirty years old. My parents were a little concerned. I asked my friend, "Are your parents concerned about the PLO and what they are doing?"

She said, "My dad tells me all the time that life

is extremely fragile. Every day he has seen situations where people walked in, they've been extremely healthy, and sixty seconds changes their life. They never saw it coming. So my dad tells me all the time, live. If there's something you want to do, go do it. Because in a blink it all changes."

Fixin' to.

This quote is on the tombstone of Brandon Lee, the famous Asian actor who is buried beside his famous father, Bruce Lee. It comes from a book called The Sheltering Sky *by Paul Bowles. "Because we don't know when we will die, we get to think of life as an inexhaustible well. Yet everything happens a certain number of times, and a very small number, really. How many more times will you remember a certain afternoon of your childhood, some afternoon that's so deeply a part of your being that you can't even conceive of your life without it? Perhaps four or five times more. Perhaps not even that. How many more times will you watch the full moon rise? Perhaps twenty. And yet it all seems endless."*

I want you to sit—you are probably doing a lot of that these days—and think about what you really want to do. Then go do it. Go do it now. Don't be a fixin' to. If this taught you anything make it to get rid of Mr.

Fixin' to. Live. Live. Because some day, maybe some day soon, the inevitable is coming.

         —The Sender

As she sat in her car, Leah looked in her rearview mirror and saw Dulcinea. And she vowed to herself that she'd stop "fixin' to" and go live a new life now.

RELIEF. ROUND TWO WAS OVER. Charlie relished an unfamiliar inner calm that things would be all right. He still couldn't see a clear pathway for how that might work out, but he just had a sense of certainty that his life and the most important elements in it, Eve and the girls, were going to be fine.

It was Thursday and the plan was to have a special family dinner together for the first time in weeks. His mind drifted to Max alone in his hospital room and Charlie felt a moment of worry . . . sadness . . . *wishing* that Max could be there with them. There was a thrill in the air and Charlie just wanted to share it with his closest people.

Family dinners can become routine. Not this one. It was as if everyone at the table knew they'd been playing a high-stakes game of some sort and were finally turning the tables. Eve cooked and the girls prepped and got everything ready. The evening had a warmth and wonder about it that was a rarity for them.

Charlie's appetite had returned a bit and whatever Eve was cooking smelled heavenly. He'd come into their room to change and had briefly lain on the bed to rest. He looked at the ceiling and hadn't anticipated the flood of thoughts that came to his mind. They swirled: the girls, the team, the cancer, Bing, Pearly, Max . . . Leah. Victory and death all bunched together so close. He didn't know what it all meant but he felt that strange confluence of feelings again. Excited and nervous. Hopeful yet harshly realistic. He just wasn't sure he liked it, but he was ready to push on into whatever life might bring.

Then as he lay there he heard it again. It was the haunting echo of something he'd been hearing for days. It was a simple phrase he'd read. It got stuck in his head like a song you can't stop hearing. *"Lessons will be tested . . . Lessons will be tested . . . "*

CHAPTER .25

WOMEN ARE LIVING PROOF of intelligent design. Charlie had three in his life to prove it. They were all sort of giddy with the delight you get when you recover something you lost. It's a rare feeling of nearly explosive relief. But there they were all together sharing it at once.

Haphak.

Charlie's daughters, Jessie and Jenny, were at once very different and very much alike. They were both beautiful girls; Jessie lightly blonde and Jenny brunette, both with coy and twinkly brown eyes. Jessie was a worker, organized and methodical and the Jenny a dreamer, full of wishes and romantic plans. Jessie taught herself to knit and speak French. Jenny would lie for hours in the back yard watching clouds. One thing they shared was a determination to have Charlie dance at their weddings. Charlie had every expectation to be there, and honestly it was about the only thing that he was totally certain about. In one of the letters the sender made reference to the fact that when cancer survivors finally go into remission, they're almost never surprised. Such was the case with Charlie. Though not totally in remission yet he was winning and he wasn't surprised.

The dinner conversation drifted around to many off-beat topics like shoe stores, music, and favorite colors. Charlie learned for the first time that Jessie loved powder blue and Jen, Alabama crimson. Charlie, in his embarrassment, admitted that he thought he'd heard that before, but never paid attention. That night he was paying close attention and remembering.

Football and the playoffs never even came up until dessert. Eve and the girls were so fired up, Charlie suggested that perhaps they could all go together to the game and cheer the Bucks. After they got Max, of course. The girls suddenly realized they'd totally forgotten to ask about the little guy. They launched into question after question and, honestly, Charlie had few answers. He soothed their curiosity the best he could. The rest would have to wait till they all met.

Then came the moment he'd been preparing for. Charlie reached down to three letters he had placed on the floor beside him.

The girls had of course known of his mysterious pen pal and had even read several of the earlier missives. So it was not a big stretch to tell them he wanted to read them one. They exchanged dad's-a-nerd smirks, then in true Cristo spirit shrugged in unison and asked him to go on.

Charlie reached down and grabbed the first letter. He opened it with faux pomp, cleared his throat and began.

It is said that General William Booth of the Salvation Army was trying to motivate his troops at the little kettle bells one Christmas. He had this long message he was going to put out on a telegram. But it was too expensive. So he shortened it a little bit. Still too expensive. So he sent out a one-word telegram to all the ringers in the entire world. It said simply, "Others."

I want you to keep teaching yourself and I am going to keep teaching myself—others. In this self-absorbed, it's-about-me world, we sometimes forget it's about others. I want you to keep teaching your team. Others. Let's keep teaching each other. Others.

—The Sender

Eve was tearing up again.

"Girls, can I ask you a favor?" Charlie said, putting the letter down.

Both girls nodded.

"That letter is about the bonds of siblings. You two are

bonded that way. We don't know what's going to happen next; we never do. But I learned a lesson: it's not about what happens to you. Rather it's about keeping your vision, working toward it with everything you have, and encouraging others. Lifting others up. If you do that for one another I'd be the happiest man on earth. Will you do that for each other, no matter what happens to me?"

The girls both flickered their soft brown glistening eyes as if they were angels themselves. That's all Charlie needed.

He reached down and pulled up two more letters.

"These are letters, girls, that I want you to read on your own. I picked them out for you as a gift, and they have messages I'd dearly love you to lock away in your heart. Will you do that?"

Charlie handed them the letters and the girls handled them as if they were the freshly scribed Ten Commandments.

Then he turned to Eve.

"I have one for you too, my dear. But I will give it to you when you can use it the most."

They all looked at each other and chuckled nervously.

"I could've used one per hour, buddy," she shot back with teary eyes. "This hasn't been easy," she added. It was a light matrimonial wake-up slap.

Charlie looked down at his hands, then gathered himself and said simply, "Thank you. I would not be here were

Kevin Elko and Bill Beausay

it not for you all. Especially you, Eve. I have three simple goals: be a great father and husband, do the work of that every day, and lift all three of you up whenever I can."

It was deathly still at the table. Nobody said a thing.

Eve swallowed hard, then rose and began clearing the table.

Friday was going to be an exciting day at school. The girls were going to leave school after lunch to go with their dad and get Max. He'd be a kick, and they couldn't wait to see him.

They each went to bed, but stayed up with their lights on. Jessie's letter went like this:

Charlie. It's me.

It's my birthday today. Just been thinking about a few things here as I'm getting older. And here's what I'm thinking as you fight your battle and win it. Here's what I think about you getting ready to get your team to go to the next step.

There is a myth that the ancient Celts in Scotland had a name for the Holy Spirit which translates into "wild goose chase." I kind of like that. You know it suggests that the Spirit of the Divine can never be tracked or tamed. It's kind of crazy, the little boxes we put the Holy Spirit into. All of us. But it can't be tracked or tamed.

I'm not sure our lives should be tracked or tamed. In Tolstoy's novella The Death of Ivan Ilyich, *it opens with a phrase that says something like Ivan Ilyich's life was most simple and ordinary and therefore most terrible.*

I hate the sound of my guardian angels yawning. I just hate it. I'm going to keep pushing it. Let's push it together. I'm going to make my prayers bolder. I'm going to make my thoughts crazier until somebody tells me that my thoughts are crazy. Then I'm going to say, "No, your thoughts aren't crazy enough."

The last seventeen years of my father's life were pretty good. We went on vacations together. We had some fun together. We went to Vegas together. When he passed away you know what I thought? It's kind of a good lesson for me. I said it's not that this man died too young—he was eighty-two when he died. He lived too late. That's what hit me.

I love this line from the theologian Kierkegaard: "And what wine is so sparkling, what is so fragrant, what is so intoxicating as possibility?" I'm going to start—me and you together—thinking outrageously.

Why not a state championship? Why not make a huge dent in cancer? Why not live all the way?

I love the Rabbi Harold Kushner. He's said so many wonderful things. I want to paraphrase one. This probably isn't right but I think he said, "I've sat at a lot of people's deathbeds. And the ones who have the hardest time dying are the ones that never really loved." I like to think of love here as really living. Really living, really big.

Here's what I'm going to get into. I am going to flirt with these ideas: Why not us? Why not dream big and even outrageous? And pray bold. Expect more. That's what I think I would text my team as they get ready to play in the playoffs. Expect more. Play harder and expect more. Let your play show that you expect more. Let your dreams show that you expect more.

Wild goose chase. I like the idea of that. His life was most simple and ordinary and therefore most terrible. I'm not going to die like that. And Happy Birthday to myself.

—The Sender

In the darkness Jess smiled as big as the moon. And she fell asleep thinking of a big life and joy and goose chases.

In the next room Jen carefully set her lamp for optimal

light and opened her letter. She was not used to reading in bed.

Hey Coach, it's me.

There's a story about a boy trying to pull a calf into the barn. He was pulling and sweating. He finally gave up because he couldn't get the calf in the barn. And a young woman came by and she just stuck her finger in the calf's mouth. The calf associated the finger with security and the sensation that the calf used to get from its mother and it followed her into the barn.

Great leaders are like that. I know people that want to shout and demand and shove their agenda down other people's throats. But caring is something really very different. It's understanding where the other person is.

You are different. I've known you for a long time now. You are different. Where you are different is you understand the wounds of your ballplayers and people around you. I personally prefer friends that have been through a divorce, have lost someone they have loved, or have lost a job or been downsized, so that they can say, "I've been there. I've been there."

Like I told you, I ain't where I want to be but, thank goodness, I ain't where I used to be!

Hey, I've been rejected. I've been fired. I've had

sickness. But let me tell you what to tell people. Christ looked at Jairus and said, "Don't be afraid." Believe. Censure that cancer. What world has that opened up for you? What people do you now understand? Someone who's been afraid. Somebody who thought they might lose a job because of their health. Someone who thought they might lose their life because of their health.

Tell them this: We all die in the end. That's not what to be afraid of. What's to be afraid of is getting paralyzed by fear and dying in the middle. *We all die in the end. Just don't die in the middle. I want to tell you what I've told you so many times. Don't waste your cancer. The world has opened up to you. Your heart has opened up to many other people because of your cancer. So I want you after this to go tell people, we all die at the end. Just don't die in the middle.*

—The Sender

Jen folded the letter and lay it across her chest. She closed her eyes and her mind drifted far away.

IT WAS A BEAUTIFUL, sun-kissed morning in the cool Alabama fall. For all its magnificence, the day started off lightning quick and never really slowed down.

This evening the Bucks would be hosting the first play-off game against the Columbia Eagles from Huntsville. It would be epic and it seemed as though the whole world was psyched.

The girls went to school early as usual, but promised to be ready to go get Max soon after lunch period. Charlie and Eve picked them up at school and had to weave through heavy traffic of media and concessionaires getting ready for the game just to exit the school property. This would be an epic day.

The girls thought Max was awesome. This kid just had a charisma about him. He seemed to bring out the best in others in the most innocent, benevolent way. He was too young to have much guile, so his unintentional wisdom always landed like a sucker punch.

Max and Grampy waited for them in the hospital turn-about. Max wore his Seminole Valley Bucks hat pulled down over his ears. He looked thinner than before, but surely it was the oversized hat.

As Max bounced in the car and hugged the girls, he waved at Charlie and asked if they were going to stop and get Popsicles. Tradition is tradition.

"Of course we can, young blood," Charlie replied.

Max huffed and snorted and laughed.

"*Young blood*. I like it when you call me that. Makes me feel like a strong guy . . . The doctor said I need to eat sugar-free Popsicles though," he added, his face falling. "He thinks I might be getting too much sugar. That's what's wrong with me."

That sounded strange to Charlie, so he asked Grampy to clarify. Grampy shrugged.

"They're not really sure what's up. But if he gets to feeling bad tonight we might have to get him back to the hospital."

In the cancer business you learn to take punches. That felt like one to Charlie, but he kept his thoughts to himself and assured Grampy he'd run them back at any time.

The girls and Max chatted amiably in the back as they pulled into the carnival atmosphere back at the high school. The school pep rally had ended and many students had stuck around to decorate the stadium and just drink in the excitement of the evening.

They pulled around back near the athletic department doors. Many gathered around the car as they saw the group arrive. Max of course was the real attraction. He emerged from the rear door of the car like a rock star among the paparazzi. Word of him had spread since his last visit. One of the students handed him a felt pen and he signed autographs. Heady stuff for such a little person who'd spent much of the last several weeks isolated on a cancer ward.

He handled it like he'd been dreaming of it.

After Max's fans dispersed, they all entered the school through the locker room doors. It was late afternoon now and nearly time for Charlie's pregame pep talk. Several students were carrying the cooler of Popsicles Charlie brought, and the group entered the team locker room. The girls stopped short, hugged Max, and promised him they'd see him after the game.

The girls each kissed his pale forehead good-bye.

"Go Bucks!" he whispered to them with a wink.

Max was well known to the boys and he received a hero's welcome. The group of young players were noticeably tense and Max's lighthearted nature was exactly the medicine they needed. He high-fived anyone who came near, and immediately began handing out Popsicles, sugar-free, and he was the perfect encouragement.

The coaches and players were happy to see Charlie too. He walked into the coaches' office and closed the door behind him. It was not long before the welcomes turned to the serious nature of the challenge at hand. Charlie couldn't have been happier to hear the game plan, discuss scouting reports, briefly watch some film, and grab some donuts provided by the boosters.

Coach Charlie had planned on talking to the team at about five. At 4:45, he excused himself and wandered to a solitary part of the athletic wing of the school to gather his thoughts. There were several interconnected rooms, joined by doors, all dark and seemingly empty.

Charlie went into one and did something he just didn't often do. He knelt and prayed out loud.

"God, the last several months of my life have been . . . well, you know. I'm grateful to be here. Tonight I feel tired and afraid. You seem to like to have me in positions like this. Whatever happens tonight, I pray that you will be here. I pray that you will let me keep focused, do my work, and help me lift the arms of these young men. You'll take care of the outcome. I'm here if you need me . . ."

Charlie wasn't in the habit of rating his own prayers, but that one sounded pretty tight.

As he rose to leave and head back in for his pep talk, he heard what sounded like groaning in the adjoining room. He stopped and strained to hear. Then again—groaning, maybe loud talking in the dark.

Fearing many sorts of trouble, he opened the door and entered the darkened room and flipped on the light. There, lying face down in the middle of the floor was Max. He rolled over and looked up at Charlie.

"Max, are you all right? What are you doing here?"

Max looked sallow and wrung out under the lights, innocently oblivious of how bad the situation looked.

"Well coach, I was eating some Popsicles with the boys and suddenly I felt very bad. So I asked them to bring me somewhere dark . . . that's what I like . . . and they brought me in here and laid me down. I hope that's OK. I was laying here and then I heard you come in and start praying next door. I thought it was a pretty good idea, so I rolled over on my tummy and started praying too. It's fun!"

Fun? All right.

"Are you OK?"

"Don't worry about me, Coach. I can take it. I got guts . . ."

Charlie was both relieved and, of course, charmed.

"Are you ready to go talk?" Max asked. "I think I can get up now."

"Be brave, my little young blood," Charlie said, reaching a hand down to lift him up. "Let's roll."

Together they strode back into the locker room for the biggest pep talk of their lives.

CHAPTER .27

IT WAS FIVE O'CLOCK and the team had gathered. Seventy-five sweaty high school guys jammed together in a locker room before the biggest game of their lives is a laboratory of craziness. Some were very quiet, half dressed, and sitting staring at their feet. Others milled around pinching, punching, or grabbing their teammates, some yelling, some singing, some guys throwing up in the bathroom stalls, everyone just trying to shake off the pressure in their own way.

Charlie asked them all to sit. They quickly sat themselves pretty much wherever they were, went silent, and waited for marching orders from their emaciated, Lazarus-looking coach.

"You fellas have been on a quite a march. It's been months in the making, coming back from a slow start when I was coaching to this magnificent turnaround under Coach Picasso."

149

The boys spontaneously erupted in applause for ol' Leatherhead. In retrospect Johnny Picasso had gotten what he wanted: the head coaching job and a shot at state. Charlie was supremely happy it worked out this way.

"Now tonight. The biggest night of some of your lives. Last week I had Andrew read you a letter before the game. Does anyone remember what was in it?"

The whole group erupted in this head-bobbing hoot, "Honi Baby!" and making this strange hand gesture. Like boys do.

Others in the group chimed in.

"Think big! Bigger circle! Big storm tonight!" they yelled.

Sheesh, Charlie thought, *this stuff really sticks.*

"Honi's my man, and I'm glad you liked that. Well, I thought since that letter went over so well I'd read you another. You guys in?"

All heads nodded.

"I got this note at a time when I needed it badly. Here goes."

On Sunday nights when I'm lying around all happy I sometimes think about my dad. I think, "My dad would love this." Sometimes I'm watching my little boy play soccer. "He's all boy," I think, "My dad would love this." Once we almost got into a fight with some-body from another team and I thought, "Whoa, my dad loved a good fight."

Paul McCartney of the Beatles was doing that one time. He was doing what I do on a Sunday night, just sitting and thinking some. He was twenty-six years old and he was wishing his mother was there. His mother died twelve years earlier, when he was just a boy. She was a nurse.

And he was thinking, "I wish my mother was here" and he fell asleep thinking about his wish to have his mother there.

He could never see his mother's face in his mem-ory. He was fourteen when she died, but still he couldn't remember her face. But his mother came to him in a dream that night. And she said to him, "Paul, let it be." He was sleeping. She said it to him in the dream. His mother's name was Mary.

He woke up. He thought she was in the room with him. It was all clear. He wrote "Let It Be" that night.

My wife, Karen, has a beautiful line, "Be where your feet are." Just be where you are right now and forget everything else. Focus on now. Be where your feet are. Let it be. I bet right now you would love to get out of that hospital and be with the mighty Bucks.

I don't blame you. But be where your feet are. Just let it be.

I so wish you were somewhere else because I love you. I wish you weren't going through this. But I thought about it and I prayed about it. Be where your feet are. Take this completely in trust that the life you go back to when this is over will be incredible. Just be where your feet are now. Just let it be.

—The Sender

"Boys," Charlie began, "you have a million things going through your heads right now. You're thinking about your parents, your friends, your girlfriends. You're thinking about this game and what's ahead of you. Some of you might be worried about these guys that are going to be across the line from you. You might be worried about how you'll look on television. You might be worried about scholarships or whether or not you'll do something great tonight. Let me just tell you that none of that—none of it—has anything to do with winning this game tonight. I'm not going to pound this into you boys; you know what you have to do. Someone throw me a shoe."

As often happens in a locker room, a shoe came hurtling from nowhere toward the coach. He caught it deftly, no-look style. Skinny, thin, and pale Charlie stopped talking and looked at the shoe now in his hand.

"Almost won the Heisman on plays like that." He smiled.

The boys cheered and laughed.

"The only thing that matters tonight is being where your feet are." Charlie waggled the shoe in the air. "When things are going great, don't congratulate yourself or look to see who's cheering you. Be where your feet are; no further ahead, no further behind. When things go bad, you make a bad play, miss an assignment, miss a block or a tackle, don't replay it over and over, yelling at yourself or your teammates. Let it be. Be where your feet are and go on to the next play. There are forces and powers and plays that will go on tonight that you have no control over. The only thing you can control is where your feet are. Be where your feet are. Now go out there, do your job, one play at a time, and let it roll! I love you boys, I'm prouder of you than you'll ever know, and I will see you on the other side."

The boys let out a roar, and it was on. They finished dressing in time for pregame, which tonight would be extended to allow for media and others to find their positions and set up for what would hopefully be a gridiron classic.

The locker room was stifling hot so Charlie retreated

back into the air conditioned coaches' room for some final strategy.

Half an hour later he emerged and got ready to begin his slow, methodical saunter to the stadium to join the girls.

Then he saw something that made him go numb. An ambulance had pulled up to the entry to the locker room, lights flashing. He could not see what was going on but feared someone might've been inadvertently hurt in the melee around the locker room doors.

As he approached he was shocked to find that his hunches were totally wrong. It was Max.

"What the—?"

He spotted Grampy in the crowd and shuffled over to meet him.

"What happened?" Charlie yelled.

"Oh, Coach, we couldn't find you so we did the best thing. He was stumbling around a bit and coughing, Popsicle juice, I think, but it looked bright like blood, so we thought we should get him back to the hospital quickly."

Charlie was stunned. This was not the way he'd envisioned the evening. As quickly as his frail body would allow, Charlie crawled up into the back of the ambulance. Max was strapped down on a stretcher looking pretty bad.

"Too many Popsicles there, buddy?" Charlie asked, putting a big fake smile on his face.

"It was kind of hot, Coach, and something happened. I puked. I think it was because everyone else was puking."

Max convulsed with a very subtle jerk.

Having seen it before, Charlie stayed focused.

"May be. I'll come and see you soon and let you know what happens here, OK?"

"OK, Coach. Tell those boys to play hard."

"I will. Be brave, my little young blood."

Max smiled weakly, then appeared to fall asleep.

Charlie was sick with worry. Nothing mattered more than Max at that moment. Nothing.

He squeezed the young boy's hand and clambered out of the back of the ambulance. Grampy was waiting.

"Max thought he might not see you, so he asked me to give you this."

In Grampy's hand was a shoe. Charlie glanced in at Max on the gurney and sure enough, one of his shoes was missing.

"He wanted me to tell you to be where your feet are. He was hoping he could be where *your* feet are, I think."

In one memorable *haphak* moment, a moment swollen with horror, Charlie had a realization he would never forget. There was a level higher than the one he'd been playing. It's the level beyond *talking* a good game. It was the level of *living* a good game. And Max was already there.

Charlie just stared breathlessly as Grampy climbed into the ambulance and they closed the door. Inside was a small boy, his boy, with one shoe. That boy was closer to death right then than life, and he meant more to Charlie than a million football championships.

Charlie was a strong man. Nobody would question that. But at that moment he went from a general commanding an elite army to a regular scared guy. Duty vanished and forces took over. The man who never cried or became weak when the pressure peaked was dissolving in it.

In the depths of his mind he heard that faint familiar phrase ringing in his head, *Lessons will be tested.*

He shoved the shoe in his coat pocket and limped toward the stadium.

Wives know things. Charlie slowly climbed the stairs to where Eve and the girls sat. The pregame had ended and fans were milling around waiting for the team intros and the kickoff. Jess and Jen warmly welcomed their dad, waving pom-poms and flags as he approached. Eve just stared him down. This wasn't her first time seeing that look in his eyes.

"What's wrong with you?" she asked when he got near.

"Something just happened. It'll be all right."

"C'mon Charlie, please! What's going on?"

"It's Max. He had some sort of a seizure or attack or something and they had to take him to the hospital. I'm a little worried."

At that moment the crowd began to howl in unison as the Seminole Valley Bucks burst through the paper banner on the field and charged to the enormous "SV" in the center. Eve and Charlie just looked at each other through the howls, mouthing words but realizing the futility of it.

When a gap in the tsunami of sound came, Eve pulled Charlie close and insisted on knowing details.

"I don't know, Eve. I just know he looked pretty bad. Let's go over after the game."

They exchanged knowing looks and Eve mercifully let it drop. She snuggled close to him and put her arms around his slender waist. Then she felt something strange in his pocket.

"What is this?" she asked, feeling around at the small lump in his coat pocket.

"It's a long story, Eve. It's Max's shoe. I'll tell you later."

"A shoe? All right, but feels like an envelope in there too."

Charlie had completely forgotten. He reached in his pocket and pulled out a letter he had planned on giving her that night before the game. In all the commotion . . .

"Last night I gave the girls letters that meant a lot to me, and I promised that I had one for you. I was going to give this to you earlier but, well, in the midst of all this I forgot. Here . . ."

He handed her the crumpled letter that smelled like dirty shoes.

"I will read it, Charlie. Mind if I wait till later?" she

asked, as the game announcer's voice suddenly boomed through the speakers, and the game began.

It was one of the most exciting moments of this whole dreadful season for the Cristos. It felt like a moral victory just to be here, in the playoffs, when just several months ago they were thinking funerals. The game was closely fought, with great defense, big dazzling plays, and enough intensity for an entire season. In the end, Seminole Valley beat Columbia-Huntsville in a nail-biter, 31–29. Their first playoff game was in the books. Two more to go and then the final . . . he hoped.

THEY PULLED INTO THE EMERGENCY entrance at the hospital shortly before midnight. Partying with team lasted way too long, but the intoxication of victory celebrations, especially after such a hard-fought important win, was difficult to resist. They were tired and covered with sweat, dried sticky Coke, popcorn dust, and chili-dog sauce.

They entered the ER and asked where Max was. They were referred to the pediatric cancer floor, but told the visiting hours were over. Having experience in these things, Charlie asked to use a house phone to contact the charge nurse for that evening.

After a brief and intense phone call, he came back to Eve and the girls and told them they'd have to come back in the morning. Charlie was told that things were not OK and he got somewhat scolded about their excursion that night.

Charlie looked worried and the girls did their best to console him. Team Cristo vowed to come back the next day.

They drove away, Charlie staring blankly out the car window.

Sometime later that night Charlie was fast asleep. Eve was restless, anxious, and nowhere near sleepy. She sat up, turned on a small lamp next to the bed and opened the stinky letter Charlie had given her at the game.

I think one area I need to keep working on is forgiveness. I don't know, everybody is walking around these days offended. A few years back, I was speaking at the Million Dollar Round Table annual meeting. And there was a woman there. Her name was Kim Phuc. When she was a little girl, she was in a famous photograph. The photo was of her running out of a village in Vietnam with her back burning from napalm. She's a grown woman now.

She's a professional speaker and her message is very simple: "My wounds healed a long time ago. Go heal yours."

Forgive.

Resentment is taking poison and expecting some-one else to get sick.

All the stuff that we've been through with other people, all the things that have been said about us— we've always just said, "Forgive." So I'm asking you to get healthy and get out of there. Because I need me a lifelong catfish. You know the parable of the catfish? The Chinese catch codfish in the Pacific and ship them live to China in these big tanks. But by the time they arrive they are all fat and soft from just sitting in that tank. So they started to put catfish in the tank to harass the cod to keep them on their toes and keep them swim-ming and keep them strong and fresh. I need a catfish. I need someone that says, "I care about you." Be my catfish. Keep me fresh. Keep me on my toes.

My forgiveness strategy is easy. I just close my eyes and say, "Send them peace." I even sometimes send them a gift. I sometimes send like a fancy pen or something like that. Sometimes I send them a book. All right, buddy. I want you to be my lifelong catfish. I need one. I need somebody that keeps me accountable, and I trust you and I love your spirit. Keep getting better, partner. I'm thinking about you and praying about you.

—The Sender

Eve leaned over and looked at Charlie sleeping by her side. She just looked at all the lines in his face, his thin neck, and splotchy bald scalp. She moved closer yet and kissed him on the forehead. For all the trouble he brought at times, she was kindling a fresh love for him. She knew at that moment that she'd forgive him and be his catfish.

THE NEXT MORNING WAS BRUTAL. In just a couple of days Charlie was going to going back for his third and, he hoped, final round of chemo. He did not expect to be back in any sort of hospital until then, but here he was standing at the nurse's station on the pediatric cancer wing of UAB hospital, facing the fiery eyes and spitfire tongues of the nursing staff.

They were really hot at Charlie and wasted no words ripping him. When Max had arrived back at the hospital the prior evening he was gravely ill. Charlie tried to explain, but nobody was listening. Their job was not to field excuses but to get to the bottom of this setback and fix it.

Charlie asked if he could see his friend.

"There's only one reason we're letting you in, Coach: Max said you were coming by and made us promise. Make it fast. And don't even bother trying to call him."

Charlie was not used to this kind of treatment, but he understood the rules. He promised he would not be long and hurried down the hall. Many of the little kids dotting the halls and playroom hooted as he went by and congratulated him on the big win. Charlie just wanted to be invisible.

He simply was not prepared for what he saw as he entered the room. This was not the scene of a minor setback. Tubes, IVs, machines, computer screens, and acrid smells screamed of something dire going on. Max was still, gazing at the ceiling.

Charlie went right to him and sat down on a chair near his side. Max rolled his head to the side and smiled. His lips were thin and gray. Dry. He tried to lick them but his leathery tongue failed him. Having been there himself, Charlie knew just what to do. Reaching for a nearby glass of water, Charlie drizzled small water droplets on Max's lips with a straw he found on the table.

Max's eyes lit and he lurched up slightly with a question, but delivered little more than a grunt.

"We won, 31–29," Charlie interrupted, smiling broadly and gently pushing his little body back down.

Max lay still, connecting the dots in his fogged mind, then burst into a smile.

"This helped, my man," Charlie continued, reaching into his pocket and holding up Max's shoe.

Max just smiled and seemed to go to sleep.

Charlie hung on to the moment, just watching Max silently. His thoughts were jumpy and worried. Then he remembered that for so long he'd been in exactly the same place. Tired, hazy, hurting, confused. He remembered weeks and weeks of discomfort and searing pain, and prayers and curses and pleas and silence from God. And nothing else.

In silence he continued, day after day begging God to be spared. And he grew dark and angry, still begging God to provide some way out, some relief. And he felt like quitting, but thanks to those letters he chose to keep believing. And slowly relief came. Not as he expected, but it came.

He remembered that in one of those letters the Sender encouraged him to ask God to make him as big and strong as an oak tree. He had him visualize the tree in all its fullness and detail. He created a beautiful tree in his mind and he believed that God would deliver it.

He looked down at Max and saw it now . . . an acorn. He'd been asking God for oak trees, and in his wisdom God sent him an acorn to grow.

Charlie vowed he and Max would become big strong trees together.

He laid his hand on Max's sleeping head and prayed for his little acorn. And he was sick with fear. This was one lesson he never expected to have tested.

He left the shoe on Max's nightstand with his cellphone number written on a napkin. He stood up and crept to the door and felt a chill in the room.

CHAPTER .32

A MOMENT-BY-MOMENT, surgical-waiting-room sort of anticipation clouded the next few days. It was all about Max, and the entire Cristo clan was caught up in it. Charlie had not heard his cell phone ring much the last few months, but this weekend it was nonstop with congratulations, encouragement, and excitement. But every time it rang anyone around perked up and looked. Was it Max? Any word?

Charlie tried to distract himself. He spent time with the girls, learning to knit and watching clouds. He'd never known what he was missing. But the thought of Max was always close by.

So it went till Tuesday when it was time to get back to being a patient himself again. The third round. Maybe this would be it. Eve drove while Charlie dreaded. The journey had a lot of bad associations for Charlie and he genuinely hated it.

"Just get through this, honey," Eve said, easily spotting

Charlie's demeanor and reservations. She reached over and gripped his hand.

"There is a lot going on now between Max and the game this week, but focus on staying strong, "Charlie Strong," and you'll whip it."

Charlie just stared ahead.

"By the way, there is something I've been meaning to ask you."

Charlie broke his stare and looked at her.

"I want to be your catfish. Can I bite you?"

Charlie stopped, thought, and then laughed. The moment became suddenly golden. It was the perfect antidote at the imperfect moment.

They arrived at the hospital and went through their admission routine, calling out most of the nurses by name. Maybe this would be the last time . . .

They walked hand-in-hand to Charlie's room and got him all set up. A group of letters had collected in Charlie's shoebox, and he quickly shuffled through the new ones. Eve had never really seen him so psyched about something. He looked up at her, smiled, then waved the letters and said, "Godsends."

Eve finished unpacking Charlie's clothes into the drawers and was getting ready to leave when a cell phone rang. At first they were not sure whose phone it was, but realized it was Charlie's. He answered it and his eyes immediately grew large. On the other end was a voice he did not expect to hear.

"Hi, Coach Cristo, this is Cinderella! *Hehehehe*!"

"Young blood! My man! How are you?" Charlie beamed. Charlie loved happy endings. His Cinderella story had come true.

"Oh I'm fine, Coach. Just being where my feet are!"

"You are something, kiddo. Are you feeling better? The last time I saw you things were not so good. I thought maybe you ate too many Popsicles."

"Oh no, Coach. I just have those spells every once in a while. They make Grampy and Grammy cry. But I can usually calm them down. They keep telling me to feel better. But you know what, Coach? I keep telling them it doesn't matter how good you feel . . . it matters how good you look and then I rub my head. *Heeeeheeeheee!*"

Charlie grinned uncontrollably, looking up and glancing at his own emaciated bald head in the mirror next to the bed.

"Look, friend," he replied, "I have to be in here for a couple of weeks, but when the Bucks make the state championship I want to be there with you. We can watch it together on TV. Is that OK?"

"Gosh, Coach. Gosh. Gosh. I will ask my nurses. I bet

they say yes. I like watching big football, and they won't care."

"This could be the biggest day, buddy. State. Can I bring Eve?"

"Oh sure, Coach. Me casa, su casa. I've been working on my Spanish with another boy here."

Wow.

"You're hotter than a five-dollar pistol, laddie," Charlie said.

"Huh . . . *a five-dollar pistol*," Max repeated quietly, almost to himself, no doubt stashing it away in his magnificent little mind for later.

Charlie chuckled through several more exchanges with Max, then his nurse called a halt. It was the medicine Charlie needed at that instant. For a moment he wasn't sure who was the acorn and who was the tree.

LESSONS TESTED. TEST PASSED. Charlie was glad he didn't have to do that again.

But there'd be more lessons. He knew that as soon as Eve left he'd have his work cut out for him. In chemo sessions past he'd always been focused on himself and his own private dreads. This time was different. He was mostly concerned about his friends at the hospital, Bing, Leah . . . and Pearly. What was up with Pearly?

A bright-red face appear at his door, interrupting his thoughts.

"Welcome back, all star!" Bing shouted.

Charlie was dumbstruck. The last time he had seen Bing, he was in a critical-care area, and he just assumed . . .

"Bing! How are you, my friend?"

"Well, I'm still here, which could be good or bad, depending," Bing said.

"Please come in," Charlie said.

Bing stepped through the door, and when Charlie got a good look at him he gasped. Bing had lost about fifty pounds and in truth, looked great.

"I thought you were a goner, buddy" he said, smiling at his own gallows humor.

"No chance, pal. You gave me that letter and it pulled me through. You mentioned you hadn't read it, and I thought, well, you might be able to use it now."

Charlie remembered the letter he'd left when he'd visited Bing upstairs. Now Bing held out the opened and partially mangled envelope.

"Good medicine there, buddy. Not sure who's sending you these, but whoa—ah . . . good stuff."

"I'll pass along the sentiments as soon as I find out who it is," Charlie replied.

"Are you going to be here long?" Bing continued in a more subdued, warm way than Charlie ever remembered.

"Thanks for asking. Week or two, or so. Last round. Then hopefully on to a happy and productive life, you know."

Bing smiled. "I'm hopeful for you, friend. Settle in and when you feel up to it, cards."

Charlie smiled at the old shark and nodded his head in acceptance.

"In the meantime, read that letter. Being in for round three, you're going to need it," Bing said, sauntering out the door. The old Bing was back.

CHARLIE ARRANGED HIS BED and got in. It was only shortly past noon and he was already beat. He reached out for the note Bing brought and pulled the worn letter out of the envelope. It was really worn . . . like a teenage love letter that gets read a hundred times.

> *All right, Coach, it's me.*
>
> *I want to talk about fighting weary. It's easy to fight when we are fresh. But how you have success in parenting, success in business, success with our health, overcoming the condition of cancer, is we learn how to fight weary.*
>
> *I know right now you can probably barely function. There was a general by the name of Gideon and he was leading the Israeli army—this is written about in Judges in the Bible. He went to the head of another*

tribe and asked, "Can you give me some bread? My men are fighting weary."

You're weary. I was listening to a general on CNN. He said in Afghanistan that his soldiers are tired. And my mind went right to Gideon. We have to learn how to fight weary.

Great boxers never train to knock you out. They are trained to cut you and then work the cut. But you know that part. Here's the part you don't know. And they are also taught to survive the assault. Some boxer will come and try to assault and go crazy. But he will box himself out.

Cancer, Charlie, will box itself out if you keep fighting weary and you survive the assault. Here comes your opponent's assault. But it was just an assault. It wasn't a victory. Your energy stayed even. That's the point. Your energy stayed steady. Survive the assault.

Fight weary. Don't just work the cut, but keep working the cut and survive the assault. Cancer has an assault to it. Parenting has an assault to it. Every relationship has an assault to it. You survive the assault and you stay steady and you stay even so people don't even know you are in an assault.

When you start to feel tired and when you start

to feel frustrated, it's a sign that you are getting close. People misread the tiredness sign and they think it means, "I'm far away; I'm not making progress." No. It's the dark before dawn. You are getting close. So you tell yourself when you are tired, "I'm getting close." Survive the assault.

I'm getting close. Fight weary. And the apostle Paul said it best because he knew about this stuff. If you do not grow weary, you will reap in due season if you faint not. That means you are getting close.

I hated that you had a couple of bad days but I love it that you are getting close. As Gideon said, fight weary. Keep going. And the whole time when you can barely function, just keep whispering to yourself, survive the assault.

—The Sender

Weary. Sleepy. Tired. Charlie was all of it. He closed his eyes and slept. On the scoreboard of life he felt as though he was finally gaining some ground. The lesson he forgot was that the score doesn't matter.

HE WOKE UP SOMETIME LATER. The sun was setting, and his first thought was that he'd missed his favorite soap. He hadn't seen it in a week or so and wanted to catch up. It would wait. He wasn't going anywhere.

His first chemo session would be bright and early the next day, so he figured he had that evening of being lucid and somewhat comfortable before the door closed again on his senses. He'd make good use of the time.

His first task was getting a note off to Max. He thought for a moment of calling him, but knew that would be forbidden. So he combed through his letter journal and found one that really connected. He knew Max would like this one.

Here's what I want you to do after today. I want you to keep on thinking about what are the steps involved with winning. Not the results of winning. I want you to keep on thinking about the steps of beating cancer. Not the results of beating cancer. I'm eating very healthy, my nutrition is right, I'm exercising, I'm daily experiencing peace. The results will take care of themselves. You'll like this: my little boy's basketball team lost their first game 44 to 4. So I brought them together before the next game. We all held hands. We said a prayer. And then I said, "Look, I'm not worried about the score. I want you to just box out all day. Do you all remember how to box out the other players with your rear end when you're rebounding? Every time I call your name, I want to see you boxing out. When we play man for man, I just want you to constantly cover your man. When that ball is loose, I want you to dive for the ball. Just cover your man. Just box out and go for the ball." That's what I told them before our game yesterday. This game we lost 34 to 5. See, this stuff works! We're getting better! Keep planting grass, don't pull weeds. Keep planting grass, don't pull weeds. That's what I want you to say because I know you are upset about being sick. But with your cancer and your team it's the same. Stay on the process. The product will take care of itself. Thirty-four to 5, Dog. This stuff is powerful.

—*The Sender*

Charlie wondered for a minute if the lesson might be beyond Max. Then he laughed quietly. *Not this kid*, he thought. The best lessons in life are the ones even a ten-year-old could get. Max would not only get it but share it. That was a guarantee.

Charlie licked a prestamped envelope, loaded up with a personal encouragement and set it in his "out" shoebox.

THE NIGHT WAS YOUNG. Dinner came and went. Visiting hours were underway and though Charlie had told the girls they needn't come to see him, he missed them like never before. Because he was not in any sort of critical emergency the nursing staff was mostly leaving him to himself, so he decided to wander out in the hall and people watch.

There had been some turnover since he'd left the prior Thursday, but some of the old faces remained. Nurses, admin personnel, and the caretaker staff. Angels in blue scrubs, every one of them. Charlie smiled and nodded to everyone. They looked at him quizzically, not entirely sure what was going on. Charlie's attitude had morphed, but sometimes reputations take time to catch up.

Then he saw a face he did not at first recognize. It was a man, a younger man who was clearly not a patient but at that moment looked as though he should be. Charlie looked at him and something was familiar. The man's eyes were red, he looked flushed and dazed. Not an altogether unusual look for a cancer floor, but a visitor?

In a flash of recognition, Charlie understood. It was Pearly's husband. He shuffled past and Charlie just stayed quiet. But his mind raced.

When it seemed appropriate, Charlie stopped a nurse and asked about Pearly. The nurse's previously animated face went slack. Her eyes, previously bright, glazed.

"Pearly died about an hour ago, Charlie. She'd been doing badly as you know, and it was her time."

Charlie was speechless. There were no words. Pearly was the first person he tried to lift up with his letters and . . . it just wasn't supposed to happen that way. Not Pearly. She was young and pretty and had babies and a happy life in front of her. He didn't really even know her but her life seemed so full of promise. He thought instantly of her husband. What must it be like, he wondered, to lose someone so close? Someone you love?

He had to talk to Eve. He was practically frantic. A crushing sadness. He excused himself from the nurse and hobbled into his room, barely able to contain himself. He grabbed his cell phone and dialed Eve. She answered instantly and Charlie exploded in sobs. He could not stop.

Heaving and heaving in a sadness he did not even fully understand. This poor girl and the loss to the world . . . her husband and her little boys. Charlie sobbed and sobbed and Eve listened, unable to do anything to staunch the flow.

When his sobbing stopped, Charlie said good night to the love of his life. He did not want to die. He did not want to hurt anymore. He wanted this all to be over and to be happy and have another shot at life.

He would get it. But lessons get tested.

As he lay on his bed thinking, there was a knock on the door and Leah came in.

"Hi, Coach," she said. "I heard you weren't doing so good, so I thought I'd come and lift your arms for you."

"Hi, hon," Charlie's voice quavered, still recovering from his anguished outburst.

"You heard about Pearly," she began, clearly not entirely sure what to say.

Charlie just slowly nodded his head.

"She was a fighter," Leah began. "She told me just this morning that you gave her a letter, and how much it helped her. I told her about my "Dulcinea" letter and she thought that was pretty neat. Then she asked me something, Charlie, that I did not expect. She said, "So, Dulcinea, what are you going to do with the rest of your life?" Coach, I did not know what to say. I told her I would try to be strong and make good choices. That's all I could think to say. And it was so pitiful that I couldn't tell her what I wanted to do with my life. I promised myself that if anyone ever asked me that question again I would have a good answer. And so, Coach, I've thought about it and I want to tell you. Will you listen?"

Charlie, mesmerized by the words of this young woman in the heart of one of his life's darkest hours, sat up, wiped his eyes, cleared his mind, and opened space for Leah to speak.

"Someday soon the inevitable is coming to all of us. I learned that from your letter. And I'm not going to wait to start living it. I'm not going to put it off. I'm not gonna be a fixin' to. I'm going to focus on living every minute of every day and never again will I put things off because I'm lazy or afraid. I will never again allow myself to be bored with my life. That's my promise, Coach, and I just want you to know that I got that from you, and it became real to me from Pearly. I thank you both."

Charlie was stunned as never before. He had no words. He just lowered his tired head, closed his eyes and, well, he prayed. In those brief seconds he thanked Pearly for what she'd done for Leah, and said a little prayer of peace and power for Leah. And he prayed for Max, and Bing, and Eve and the girls. He prayed for Pearly's husband and boys and—

He'd gone to sleep praying and woke with a jerk. He felt so guilty.

He lifted his head, and Leah was gone.

HE LAY ON HIS BACK looking at the ceiling, feeling as emotionally whipped as if he'd been through another week of chemo. He hoped Leah wouldn't be offended. That was the furthest thing he'd ever dream of doing to her. He was suddenly in that chemo state of alert but tired. He sat up and wandered over to the chair sitting in the corner that visitors always used. He sat down, still somewhat stunned by Leah and the aftermath, and just looked about. The box of his letters from the Sender was on a nearby coffee table. Curious, he bent over, retrieved the box and began shuffling through the letters. Some were old and opened, others new and ready for reading.

He was tiring already and in need of some comfort. He knew a letter—the right letter—would find its way to him. So he blindly reached into the unread pile of letters and grabbed an envelope, then another and another, like he was choosing a card from a shuffled deck for a card trick.

He settled on the "right" one, opened it, and starting reading.

I was reading 2 Kings 4 in the Bible. It's a story about a woman whose son died. And she wasn't just his natural mother. She was also his spiritual mother. See, a natural mother, when a son dies, after they have tried every remedy, every doctor, everything they can think of, they just bury the kid. But a spiritual mother, they don't quit. There are natural football players and there's spiritual football players. There's natural husbands and spiritual husbands. We can go on and on.

She just wouldn't quit. So the boy died. What did she do? She said, "Fetch me a donkey, I'm going to see the Prophet." So she's riding to see the Prophet and the Prophet knew she was coming and he sent someone named Gehazi to meet this woman on the road.

And this whole message today is going to center around what I'm going to say next. This fella Gehazi asked this woman, "How are you?" I want you to listen to the answer. She said, "It is well."

She lost her son and all she said was, "It is well."

Alabama is losing to Texas A&M by twenty points. Texas A&M misses a field goal. One of the Alabama players is screaming on the sideline, "You are going to want that point back before this game is over." They are losing twenty to nothing at the time. That kid was walking around on that sideline going, "It is well." That's a spiritual ball player. His spirit was lifted. He was believing totally against the current of the situation. Alabama fought all the way back and lost on the last play of the game.

The fool depends on reason. You have to give them some reason to be happy. But the really spiritually-centered person doesn't need a reason. They just lift their spirit.

I believe that every single person who has ever beaten cancer, as soon as they had absorbed their diagnosis, started walking around saying, "It is well."

You have to start saying, "It is well." So your spirit can hear you say, "It is well." Then your spirit starts telling your body, "It is well." And your body gets confused and says, "I think we are well." You know what? Everybody expects cancer patients to crack. But surprise, it's well. I know that people are expecting me to just quit on bad situations, walk out of this job, walk out of all this. But surprise! It is well. I know people are expecting me to be so nervous that I couldn't function. It is well. No matter what happens, pause and say, "It is well."

In USA Today *today, they show a picture of somebody in the stands, looks like some wild, crazy person holding up this sign that says, "Keep Calm and Play Dead." I want to get a new sign for somebody to hold up: "It is well." Even when Gehazi came to her. Oh, and by the way, her son lived again. It is well.*

I want you to walk around just whispering, "There's a plan for me." And in between those, "It is well."

—*The Sender*

Charlie lay the letter on his lap like he'd been doing dozens and dozens of times over the last months, closed his eyes and thought, *It is well.* He wanted so badly in that moment to go lift Pearly's young husband's arms and proclaim, "It is well!" But at that moment that poor man surely just wanted to be left alone. Sometimes we all just need to hurt. Maybe later. It is well.

Moments passed as Charlie thought, then Leah came back into the room. Charlie opened his eyes and immediately began apologizing for dozing off. Leah cut him off.

"No worries, my friend. I know what you were doing. You lifted me up, and now I lift you up."

Charlie relented on the guilt, looked at Leah, and with eyes full of love and exhaustion, said simply, "It is well."

CHEMO COMMENCED the next morning and with it the days of chronic mental blur and discomfort. The pain starts in your joints then moves all over you, like a giant body headache. You never adapt to it, ever.

Charlie still struggled with his sadness about Pearly. What was the point of all this? he wondered. He knew better than most how to extract lessons out of dire circumstances, but nevertheless, this one bothered him. He tried to remember all the lessons he'd learned, hoping to glean some sort of relief from it. On this day there was none to be found. Some days the lessons were clear and fulfilling, other days hidden, tantalizing, and frustrating.

The week went fast. He was vaguely aware of his team's march through the playoffs and it really didn't register until Saturday morning when a nurse told him his team had won again. They'd beaten the almost unstoppable Lee Generals of Montgomery. Through the veil of drugs, the nausea, the unbelievable fatigue, and the body aches, he was so happy. Actually, he was overjoyed. If he only had the energy to scream and jump. He vaguely remembered what that felt like.

He had a few days' reprieve and his trippy mind cleared a bit, long enough to get some work done: letters, visiting others on the floor, and watching his soaps. He got a visit from his boys on the team and they were ecstatic. They told him with great excitement how, unlike the first playoff game, they blew these guys off the field. "One more win," they kept repeating to keep focused. Win the upcoming Friday-night game against the McGill-Toolen Yellowjackets from down in Mobile and they were in the state championship. Charlie would be in an opium haze that night, but he promised them he'd be there in his heart.

Charlie was due to be released the following week in time for the state championship, if they got by the Yellowjackets.

"Boys, I'll be there with you, and I'll give you the greatest pep talk you've ever heard, and then I'm going to watch the game with Max. I promised him we'd watch you fellas win it all."

The boys all nodded in unison, enthused that Coach would be with their adopted team mascot and with them too. They of course asked about Max and apologized about what role they might or might not have played in his set-back. Charlie did his best to assuage their concern and assured them that Max would be fine.

"Just get to the championship game, guys, and that will be *the* memory you'll carry away from this season." Charlie had a twinge of hesitation, like maybe he just told his boys something dishonest. He'd been through so much, so many memories and experiences and highs and lows, that honestly, it wasn't about football anymore. This season was about so much more. They would each have to choose what was most important to take with them.

The players high-fived their sickly coach and left. That place, the whole floor, felt better from their presence.

The mail came later that morning and Charlie waited excitedly. But his excitement would fade quickly. There was a letter from the Sender, but a returned envelope to Max too. A chill ran through Charlie. It was simply stamped, "Return to Sender," evidently by the post office. Charlie was certain there'd been a mistake so he immediately read-dressed the letter in a new envelope and resent it.

He tried to forget the error and move on, but something had changed and Charlie just couldn't get comfortable with it. He suddenly remembered the new letter he got from the Sender, and dug through the pile of new mail to find it.

He opened it up. It was a very short letter.

Sunday night, Coach. I don't know, sometimes on Sunday nights, I don't know exactly why but I get to thinking about my dad. My dad was a Marine, I think I told you, and he lived a pretty good life. I miss him. A little girl wrote me a note when he passed away. The little girl, Franny Natelle, is my daughter Claire's little girlfriend. They were both ten at the time. She did not know my name so she called me Mr. Claire. She said, "I really don't believe somebody grows up until they lose a parent." This is from a ten-year-old. And then it said, "Sorry you had to grow up."

I guess you grow up when you lose a parent. And I guess you grow up when you get cancer. You grow up when, like a lot of my friends, you lose your wife or child or best friend to cancer. Sometimes it's God's way of growing us up.

—The Sender

Charlie sank a little bit. Until Pearly he hadn't thought a lot about the death of someone you actually know. None of us really have to face pointless death very often. And it did grow him up a bit. But he didn't like any of it and in some ways still found it such a waste. But God will grow you up one way or the other and he seems to do it for his reasons, not ours.

Charlie thought of Max, lying in a bed much like his, with the sounds and smells and feelings just about like his. And he worried for the little man. He worried like a friend, like an admirer, like a coach . . . and probably like a dad. That little acorn needed to summon something inside of himself that only a cancer survivor can know. It's a special sort of grit and faith and vision and tenacity. Everyone probably has it, but cancer fighters need to choose it, minute by minute, second by second if necessary.

Charlie had been thinking of that lesson quite a bit. When you have cancer you don't feel like doing much. You have to choose to do things. You don't feel like monitoring your attitude; you have to choose it. You don't feel like drinking liquids, you have to choose to. You don't feel like being nice to your visitors, you have to choose to.

It's all about choosing despite how you feel.

Charlie whispered a quiet prayer that Max would find it within himself to choose. Nobody could choose for him. Charlie suddenly got clammy and terribly agitated, as sometimes would happen. *Must be the drugs.*

CHARLIE HAD DOZED AGAIN and awakened to Bing's big, red, smiling face sitting in the visitor's chair, just staring at him. He wanted to scream out loud, thinking that maybe he was transported to some kind of clown hell, but he regained his bearings and composure. Bing just smiled and said, "Welcome back, Buttercup!"

This was déjà vu, and not a good one. Charlie wasn't in the mood for Bing's style and begged off Bing's impromptu visit with a request to meet later. "I'm just not in the mood, Bing."

Bing leaned back in his chair and smiled. "Your choice, Coach," he chirped. "Live in the vision or live in the circumstances, you choose."

As he rose Charlie stopped him.

"What did you say? That sounds pretty philosophical for a guy like you."

He'd heard that great line in a letter and was somewhat

shocked that Bing had remembered.

"It was in some of your letters, Coach. Aussie yachters and listening to audiotapes is the one that comes to mind. You don't remember? You're the king of letters, buddy; I thought you knew them all."

The old irritating Bing was never too far away, and though Charlie was tired, he asked Bing what in the world he was talking about.

"I'll bring the letter. In the meantime, I just wanted to know if you'd want to be in my fantasy football league. I need someone smarter than the old ladies down the hall to play against. I'll even let you have Joe Namath." Bing chuckled at his own joke. "You in?"

Charlie was tired, very tired. He replied, "Kinda lost interest, Bing. But bring me that letter."

"Suit yourself, Coach. But you should think about this. You could make some money, you know. And Broadway Joe . . . whooooweee!"

"Thanks, Bing."

"I'll bring the letter, big guy. By the way, it's great to see you doing so well." Bing just beamed, and Charlie had no idea why. Bing waddled out the door and left Charlie thinking about what he'd said.

"Vision or circumstances. It's your choice."

CHARLIE FELT BAFFLINGLY TORN. He did a mental check of all his key systems: Health . . . getting there. Heart . . . check. Family . . . check. Personal peace . . . check. Focus . . . check. The team . . . off the charts check. Max . . .

Charlie just stared out into nowhere, not sure what to think or do. He felt like another test was upon him and he wouldn't feel better till he found out what was up with little Max. He wanted to support him in some way, any way, just talk to him and pick him up, but nothing doing.

He felt a little surge of anxiety so decided to walk off his concerns. He headed out into the hall and as he rounded the corner Lisa, his angel nurse, ran past. She was moving quickly, but as she whooshed by she shoved an envelope into Charlie's stomach, running-back style. Charlie took the letter and lurched forward a step or two and struck his Heisman pose.

Lisa was in a good mood and said, "You keep getting

better and I'll let you throw me some passes in the rec room, honey. That letter is from Bing. I guess I'm the mailman now."

Charlie smiled and kept walking toward the open-air deck at the end of the hall, feeling suddenly energized.

The deck was empty. The day was gorgeous. Charlie felt pretty good, considering the short walk down the hall tired him a bit. Nothing new at this point in chemo. He sat in the sun for a few minutes, only what was allowed, then moved under an awning in a very comfortable cool spot.

It was a great spot to encounter a lesson from God.

Years ago in the America's Cup, the Australian team was down under. Year after year they missed the chance to even participate in the Cup finals. And this was a point of big national embarrassment because they take great pride in their competitive seafaring skills. So they went home and listened to a positive mental attitude recording, three times a day, three times a day for four years. It was a recording of affirmations of them winning the race. They competed the following year and won the America's Cup, the first non-American club to win the Cup in its history at that time.

When a reporter asked the captain if he was surprised, the captain just looked at him. He said,

*"Surprised about what?" "About winning the race,"
the reporter replied. The captain surprised the reporter
with this reply. He said, "We already won it five thousand times. What's the big deal?" They'd already won
that race five thousand times in their minds. You either live in vision or you live in circumstance.*

*Every day I want you to take time to see yourself
in complete health. Vital. Strong. Keep on seeing it
and I want you to chant this as you chant that God
has a plan for you. Let's add a second part. "Therefore,
I will live in vision, not in circumstance."*

—*The Sender*

A cool fall breeze grazed Charlie's cheek as he looked
up, as if he'd been brushed by a passing flock of wild geese.
He glanced around and felt a sudden peace. He had a peace
that the vision he'd been given was real and clear. And in
those few seconds that it took for the breeze to skim his
cheek he became clear again about his mission, his desire to
do the work, and his choice to lift up others at any cost. He
decided to be the captain that tells his crew five thousand
times that they can win it.

He let his mind think about his crew. Eve and the girls,
all the staff at the hospital, his football team, and fellow

coaches. And Max. With shocking quickness the dread returned. He felt paralyzed. He tried to choose confidence and certainty, but he was failing. When he finished chemo next week, seeing Max would be the first stop he'd make.

THE WEEK SLID PAST in that sodium pentothal kind of way. The doctors had hit him with a very aggressive dose of chemo and it really rocked Charlie's body. The drugs to ease the effects of the chemo made it all a blur right through game night. All that week he'd done what he could to communicate with the coaches and captains, but his ideas were mostly unusable and everybody knew it. He just wanted to lift their arms in five thousand ways. And he did try.

Friday night came and with it the ebullience of the hospital staff watching the Seminole Valley Bucks beat McGill-Toolen to make it into the state championship game. Charlie slept in a chair by the TV. When he woke up, winning is about all he could comprehend. The Bucks made it into the high school Superbowl and so had Charlie.

He spent the rest of the weekend recovering, getting the druggy cobwebs cleared out and getting ready to go home.

He would be released in a few days in guarded remission, and ready to pick up his life again. His cancer was doing what remitted cancer does, and so the long hide-and-seek battle against this terrible enemy went on.

Though the weekend had been a hazy party for Charlie, the hit that came Monday morning was brutally clear to him. The letter he'd sent to Max was returned for the *second* time. Charlie immediately put in a call to the hospital. Something was really not right, and he was driven to get to the bottom of it.

Unlike previous contacts, he was bluntly turned away. He wondered if perhaps he was somehow being blackballed because of what happened the night of the football game. He hoped not. He asked and all he heard was long list of reasons for no contact including HIPAA, the wishes of the family, in the best interest of the patient, and so on. Charlie was nearly mad with frustration, but settled himself and decided to make a personal visit just as soon as he got released.

That could not happen fast enough. He tried to comfort himself by making final visits to his friends, including Bing, Leah, Lisa, and others. He shared some encouragement, his three levels ideas, and great stories to all who would listen. Charlie was a changed man. The next couple of days went well and Charlie was released to Eve on Wednesday.

All the while thoughts of Max haunted him. He packed his things but kept out two unopened letters to share with Max. He and Eve said their good-byes and left the hospital for what they hoped was the last time.

THEY WENT DIRECTLY to the UAB Pediatric Cancer Center. The ride was preoccupied and a little tense. Eve was noticeably relieved that Charlie was coming home for good, but, like Charlie, very concerned about his little man. She too had tried to reach out to him in the hospital but was brusquely refused contact. They parked near the front of the hospital in a handicapped space, and entered the front door as usual.

They were met by Grampy and Grammy, sitting by themselves in the lobby of the great hospital. They both immediately rose and met Eve and Charlie with warm hugs and stressed smiles.

They explained that Max had mysteriously undergone some extreme changes in his blood, and that it had nothing to do with the football game. Max, they shared, was a crack baby, and his blood and immune system were severely compromised in complicated ways nobody fully understood.

They apologized to Charlie about the way he'd been treated, and Charlie did his best to hide the strange terror he felt for his young friend. Grampy explained that seeing Max was simply not an option, but maybe later in the week.

Charlie grimly accepted the reality, then told Grampy that he'd promised Max he'd watch the game with him that Saturday night.

"I pray we can do something like that, Coach," he said, trying to be upbeat. "I will arrange it and you come. I will be here."

Charlie relented, something he wasn't used to doing, but promised himself he'd watch that game with Max on Saturday if he had to bring the Marines with him. He felt like he had so few options. He was blockaded at every turn. Charlie felt like he'd been released from one prison then shoved into another one. Only this one, Max's prison, was in some ways much worse.

The car ride home started quiet. But Charlie was beside himself with concern. Then seeing the two unopened letters for Max lying on the console of the car, Charlie suddenly needed to talk. His mind whirled into a frantic gear.

Eve drove quietly, not sure how to interpret this strange kind of talk from her Charlie. She made room for his nervous chatter.

"I'm not sure what you mean by all this, Charlie. Mind explaining?"

Charlie charged into an impassioned explanation of many of the things he'd learned in his letters from the Sender. He'd clearly studied these lessons, learned them, been tested, and passed. She was truly impressed by how deftly he skipped around the subtleties of the new message he now seemed to own. She glanced over at him and saw, well, a new man. Thinner, withered, she thought, noticeably flushed and bald, but stronger in so many ways. Ways that mattered. What he'd lost during chemo could be grown back. What he'd gained was immeasurably more valuable. What he'd gained was a heart and spirit that money can't buy.

They arrived home and Charlie slowly clambered out of the car, still talking nonstop about one fruitful idea after another. They unpacked the car, and Eve grabbed the two letters on the console, intending to put them in Charlie's study. Charlie kept chattering away, lost in his thoughts. As they walked up the sidewalk Eve grabbed Charlie's hand in midstride and gently yanked, breaking him out of his nervous trance. She turned him gently and kissed him hard on his now-silent lips. She told him that she loved him. She loved the new man. She was grateful for the chance to begin anew, even under the poorest circumstances. Despite the pain and uncertainty that hung over them now, she drew a breath and thanked God for the opportunities that now awaited them.

No matter what awaited them.

IT WAS A SPRAWLING orange-and-brown fall week. The colors in the trees and the coolness of the air drew nonstop sighs. But like the puffy clouds that made the bright sun flicker on and off, Charlie's mood could go sunny one moment and dark the next. This was one of the biggest weeks of his life. The Bucks had climbed the mountain against all odds and now stood on the precipice of true greatness. But dread was constantly in the back of his mind. Max. He tried to focus on helping the team, thinking good thoughts, practicing his winning on three dimensions. The further into the week he went the harder it all became.

The schedule of the week would be unusual, of course. The championship game was going to be played in Tuscaloosa at the legendary Bryant-Denny Stadium. He would meet the team there in the afternoon, give them a pep talk, then travel an hour back up to Birmingham to watch the game with Max. He'd heard no word back from

Grampy about watching the game on TV with Max, but he was determined to make that happen. After watching the game on TV, he would travel back to Tuscaloosa to join with the team in an after party that was being planned at the Bryant Conference Center, named for legendary hall-of-fame coach Paul "Bear" Bryant, in the middle of the beautiful Alabama campus.

Charlie made a quick call to Grampy to find out what was up with Max. He was sent to voice mail, and he gulped hard. Twice. Something kept bubbling up from within him and he didn't like it at all.

Charlie was almost grateful for the distraction of the game and planning what needed to be his finest motivational speech ever. He went back through all the letters that had so inspired him over the last months, looking for just the right gem with the right message for this moment. After some looking and thinking he found what he believed would be the perfect message. A message that would fill the gaps, cross the *T*s and dot the *I*s, and be the final message that might help raise the arms of his boys and push them to victory.

Sometimes you are the right person at the right time. Charlie sensed it and prepped himself to be the right person that afternoon in Tuscaloosa.

CHAPTER .44

CHARLIE AND EVE ARRIVED very early that Saturday morning to a campus dressed in her fall best, splendid, colorful, and festive by any measure. The Alabama Crimson Tide were playing away this day so the best of the Alabama high school football elite essentially had the entire campus to themselves. Everyone felt wonderful by any standard, with nerves to match.

Still no word from Grampy. It only added to his anxiety.

Charlie swore he was more nervous about all this than when he himself played, so many years ago. The team was totally prepared and excited about their chance to stun the world. They would be facing the all-time Alabama powerhouse Hoover Buccaneers. Bucs vs. Bucks. But that was about as close a comparison as most people thought this game would be. This was David and Goliath. The Hoover Bucs, the perennial champs, against the long-dormant but surging Seminole Valley Bucks.

Truth is, most people anticipated a blowout.

Everybody except those kids in the locker room. Every one of them had a flame in him, a flame he protected and nurtured and believed in. They'd been believing in it since Charlie left for chemo and no amount of doubt or challenge or difficulty was going to snuff it out. They'd been battle tested and were ready.

He and Eve had spent some time early in the afternoon with the team and promised to be back later for his pep talk. Then Charlie did something he'd never done before: he and Eve borrowed an athletic department golf cart and went on a reverie tour of the campus. They reminisced about their undergraduate days, told stories, laughed, and both were suddenly years younger. It was the perfect reprieve.

At 4:45, they headed back to the athletic facility. As he entered the building Charlie got a text, his first of the day. All it said was, "Please come to the hospital as quickly as you can." It was from a phone number he did not recognize. The ominous message turned the idyllic afternoon suddenly dark. He was hoping all the arrangements were in place for watching the game with Max, so this text was . . . concerning.

Coinciding with the text, Charlie and Eve were immediately swept up in the energy of the locker room hubbub.

It was five o'clock. Charlie tried to put the message out of his mind and focus on the task at hand.

In the locker room Coach Picasso blew his whistle and told the boys to have a seat. There was a calm intensity in the cavernous Alabama locker room. The feeling was quite unlike anything those boys had felt in their lives. Standing on the enormous script A in the center of the room, Johnny Picasso shared a few words, then asked for their spiritual mentor and leader, Charlie Cristo, to come and share a few of his now-famous words.

Charlie was waiting off to the side near the coaches' suites when the explosion happened. It was a level of pandemonium Charlie clearly did not expect. The boys screamed, whirled towels, shirts, and equipment in a total frenzy. It was as if all the emotion of a wholly emotional year climaxed in one prolonged moment of bedlam. Emotion had gotten these boys here, and clearly emotion would carry them out.

Charlie, somewhat stooped and always hobbling, took center stage in what would need to be the performance of his life. The raucous hooting and celebration went on for a full five minutes. When it died down, Charlie began turning in a small circle, looking each and every player in the eye as they surrounded him. He was silent for several long minutes, eye-to-eye with every player.

"Very few people in their whole lives will feel what you are feeling right now," he began. "Very few people know what it's like to be the best of the best. Very few know what it takes to compete for the top. Very few will ever be champions. It's rare air, boys, and I hope you are breathing it deeply—every single breath of it." He paused. "No one else but us thought we'd get here. And yet here we are. Together. Facing what will be the fight of our lives."

The room had a subdued hum. Just the buzz of the overhead lights.

"I have learned many lessons over the last few months. I have learned that pain instructs. I have hurt, and learned, and been tested, and passed all the tests . . ."

The boys suddenly hooted and clapped.

"I may not look it guys, but I am hail and hardy. Happy, strong, proud—and I'm full of something right now that I'm bursting to tell you."

The boys began their raucous shouting again. Charlie raised his frail hand to ask for silence. In moments they hushed again.

"And now, fellas, it's your turn again. You too have had pain, learned lessons, been tested, and passed all the tests."

A crescendo of sound began again, but this time the captains, led by Andrew, the quarterback, silenced the crowd with whistles.

Leadership is everything at moments like this.

"I learned something I want to share right now. You will win tonight because you win on three levels. First, you see it. I call this the spiritual, but you see what you need to do to win, you visualize it, you become absorbed in it. Second, you get out there and do the work. You do your job. And no matter what's happening around you, you remain focused on your job. You block, you tackle, you focus on the very small area right in front of you and own it. And lastly, you win for each other. Listen to me carefully: winning has nothing to do with football. Winning has to do with fighting in the trenches with your brothers. Focusing every single fiber of your being on your job and having your brothers' backs. I expect Hoover to bring their A game tonight. I expect them to be great. But I know you guys. I know you are great too. What separates us? What separates us is this."

Charlie reached out to a player seated close by and grabbed his hand, not like a handshake, but like brothers holding hands. Then he reached out his other hand to another player, and in so doing encouraged everyone to hold hands.

"This, boys, is what makes miracles happen. With each other we cannot fail. Without each other we haven't got a prayer. Don't play this game for your parents or your school or your girl or your legacy. Play this game for the guys you're holding hands with right now. We win together, we lose together—but never forget this moment, ever. Let it burn its way into your mind and never forget that we win . . . we win . . . WE WIN. It's about us. Our team. Our heart. Let nobody ever say that they did anything alone here tonight. Let them always say "*WE* did something great here tonight." And as somebody once said long ago, let those timid souls sleeping back at home tonight consider themselves cursed and ashamed that they were not here with us brothers, we band of brothers, fighting together on this battlefield here tonight."

Silence. Intensity. And just as suddenly came a strange, emergent form of human connection that nearly defies words. The boys forged themselves into steel in that moment. The tempering would come next. And the testing would go on the rest of their lives. Young people held together on a collision course with destiny—ready in every way they could imagine, yet scarcely aware of the reality of what was about to unfold.

Charlie nearly wept as he looked into the eyes of his young warriors. He, the grizzled and gritty warrior knowing all too well what lay ahead. He feared for them. He envied them. He hurt for them. He loved them.

Cancer had changed Charlie, and he was a better man for it.

He continued. "Tonight we have a vision for what we want to achieve. There are going to be a million distractions out there. I want you to focus on one thought. I want you to keep saying, "We can play this in our vision, or we can play this in the circumstances." You see, boys, I learned that lesson in the last few months, vision or circumstances. Every day I was in chemo I had to make a *choice*: live in the vision or live in the circumstances. I *chose* the vision. I did not feel like living in the vision—I felt like collapsing and giving up. But I *chose* the vision, and now I'm here. Tonight, I want you to *choose* the vision. That crowd out there, they think it's their job to get in your head. Vision or circumstances. *Choose* vision. The radio and media—circumstances. *Choose* vision. The big-name opponent—circumstances. *Choose* vision. Stay on the vision."

Not a word was breathed. Not an eye blinked. Not a body stirred.

Charlie motioned to his four captains. He called them out by name.

"Andrew, stand. Jonathon, Bobby, stand. Winston, stand please."

Charlie turned to the team.

"These are your leaders, guys. They've been here for you. They've led you. They are you. And you are them. It's game time. There is no moment in the rest of your life that you'll remember quite like this one. And these four guys are going to lead you into this epic moment."

Hoots and high fives began.

"It's time to hunt. We are the eyes and ears for you. You are the teeth. YOU ARE THE TEETH! You are going to hunt for everyone—in this crowd, at home, and forever into the future—who will hear about this game. You are going to fight for everyone that can't possibly fight for themselves. Bite hard. No mercy. Bite hard! Let's hunt!"

The crescendo in Charlie's voice brought the simmering team to full boil. Charlie grabbed his boys with his frail arms and hugged. His body was weak but he had the heart of a lion. And the boys felt it. And the boys became it.

CHAPTER .45

EVE DROVE CHARLIE as fast as she could north toward Birmingham. They listened in on the radio to the play-by-play of the game. Though he was beset with conflicting emotion about leaving his team, this was Max's night and he'd made a promise. He was not sure what he might find when he arrived.

Thirty minutes into the drive to Birmingham, his Bucks were getting thrashed. The Hoover Bucs were a machine. It was 14–0 in the first three minutes of the game, and Charlie felt sick.

"Vision or circumstances," he repeated to himself over and over. He was hoping his boys were doing the same thing. These were some mighty powerful circumstances.

As they rolled into the parking lot of the hospital Charlie was in the middle of a bad, bad dream. His team was being shellacked back in Tuscaloosa. His little friend Max would be crushed. Charlie tried to focus on the important things, but he was failing miserably. He just wanted to get up to see Max for a friendly face amid this disaster. Max would give him perspective, even if he didn't know what that meant.

Charlie glimpsed something out of the corner of his eye as he and Eve entered the front door of the hospital. It looked like an old lady, and possibly another person, sitting in a car in a handicapped spot with her hands cupping her face. In a short glance he thought it looked like a sobbing old lady and somebody trying to comfort her.

Charlie's gut flipped. He didn't know why really. It just did.

The hospital atrium was empty and deathly quiet. Charlie was seized with a moment of surprise. One hour in the middle of pandemonium in Tuscaloosa and the next in the eerie quiet of a hospital in the evening. He felt suddenly that he was where he was supposed to be.

He approached the desk and asked to see Max for their prearranged visit.

"Please wait here, Coach," the receptionist replied quietly.

Life can change in moments. This was to be one of Charlie's moments, a test to measure all tests.

An elevator door opened and out stepped Sharona. Charlie felt a burst of excitement, then dread that perhaps she was here to get rid of him. For the moment, Charlie could not even remember her name.

She walked to a sitting area and motioned Charlie and Eve to join her.

As Charlie braced himself for the riot act, she began softly sobbing. Charlie was caught completely off guard. Though his entire life the last few months had been spent dealing with sobbing, emotional wrecks, this crying was a total confusion. Nurses don't cry, right?

In a moment, the stark and horrifying truth.

No words were needed. Her faraway eyes told the whole story. Something in them was dead.

"Max is . . ." she said, dissolving into heartbroken sobs.

Charlie felt nothing. No way. Not possible. None of this is possible, he thought. Then came the overwhelming wave of reality. This was no joke. Eve stood and walked away quickly.

Charlie stared, then feeling an intense need to be alone, rose and wobbled to a nearby bathroom, which he could barely see through watery eyes. He entered and locked the door behind him. He went to the sink and lay his head down in it, bent over and shaking. Then he felt it coming. A giant, unstoppable, unfiltered purge of pain.

Charlie could hold it no longer. The horror of this

meat-grinder disease was too much. His innocent Max snatched. The gut-splitting reality hit now with full force. Charlie heaved and swallowed, gripped and heaved again. No use. What was inside had to come out and it was ugly and hard. His body took over and he shook with a hard palsy. And held on to the only thing he had to hold: himself. Desolation and emptiness doesn't come in any heavier doses.

Charlie held himself over that bathroom sink, pouring out bitter, hot swells of tears. He just couldn't get it all out. He gagged. Maybe it never would all come out. Gigantic waves kept pushing out. This was not happening. This was not possible. When one wave stopped another started. He couldn't stop them. He did not want to stop them.

He sobbed and sobbed without control or self-consciousness. The emotion came now, wave after wave. He was lost in his own world of confusion, anger, bitter questioning, and tired, wrenching pain coming from places in his heart he did not know he had. It was way worse than chemo. Way worse. And Charlie could not stop the dreadful, hot tears. He did not want to stop. He could hear them falling heavy in the sink before him and he did not care. He did not want to feel better, he did not want comforting, he did not want hope.

Where was God when I needed him the most? This was Charlie's final exam. He was failing and he did not care.

He just needed to weep for his poor little man Max. For the life and the bond that was so cruelly killed. Just shut up and cry. That's all he could do. And he did.

One of Charlie's true life treasures was gone.

By the time Charlie and Eve arrived back in Tuscaloosa, half time was just underway. The mighty Bucks were being flattened, 24–0. It was an ugly beating. Charlie had nothing to say. Nothing. He was empty, lonely, shocked, and emotionally destroyed.

He sat in the car for long moments, listening to the radio as the first half of the game wrapped up. He just stared. Eve reached over and grasped his arm.

Eve. He hadn't even thought of her. The entire drive was a numb blur.

"I'm sorry, baby," was all he could say and they held each other and cried more. Their emotional banks were badly overdrawn, but the tears kept coming from somewhere.

As Charlie leaned over to hold Eve his knee bumped the glove box and it popped open. Lying there was an old envelope covered in crayon scrawls. It was the letter Max loved and gave back to Charlie. Charlie nearly dissolved, but held it together. There was work to do. In his depths he wondered if maybe there might be a message that could help with the titanic and hopeless half-time talk he needed to give his young warriors. He asked Eve if she'd give him a moment to read the letter and collect his thoughts.

When she'd left the car he opened the letter and read carefully. To his surprise, which should have been no surprise, it was exactly what he needed. *Thank you Max*, he thought. He shoved the letter back in the glove box, took a deep, cleansing breath, and headed for the locker room.

IT WAS DEATHLY SILENT in the locker room. Shock and awe. Blood, sweat, and fear on every face. They were being mauled, and it was Charlie's turn to talk for the last time. He decided not to mention Max. Even the thought of his name made Charlie's stomach quiver and tears leap to his eyes. He held it down, asked the boys for quiet, and rose among them.

Charlie opened with the most unexpected line of all time.

"Pain instructs, boys. What did you learn?"

Nobody said a word.

"I'm sure you don't want to go back out there and go through that again. So let's not. Let's start over. And let's focus on one simple thing. I heard a story I'd like to share. In Africa . . ." he began, and the boys seemed to settle down. "In an African country there was a tribe of people in which all the parents had been wiped out by AIDS. The grandparents had to raise the babies, and they were at the end of their rope. The government was overwhelmed by the health crisis, and there was little help at hand, so they were all alone and had to figure it out themselves. The problem was that there was absolutely nothing they could do. Nothing. As elders gathered to discuss their endless problems, one of the men stood and addressed the crowd. "We have no hope, and there is nothing any one of us here can do. So whenever I see any of you in the street from now on, I'm not going to say, 'How are you?' I'm going to say, simply, 'I'm strong if you're strong. Are you strong?' and you are going to respond, 'I'm strong.'"

Charlie started going around the room, saying to each of the boys, "I'm strong if you're strong. Are you strong?" And each of the boys responded, "I'm strong," louder and in more unison each time.

Then he asked them to reach over and grab the arm of their neighbor and lift it up. "I'm strong if you're strong."

And something began that very moment in that locker room in the late fall of that crazy football season. The boys began lifting one another up in ways they'd never done before.

"Boys, when you get down in the next half, lift one another's arms and say, 'I'm strong if you're strong. Are you strong?'" And the boys in that locker room replied as a unit,

"I'm strong!" It was so loud, so resounding, that Charlie could barely stand. His young warriors. Fighting to the end. Fighting for their lives. Fighting for the life of a young kid who was already gone. And fighting for everyone who has ever been down, beaten, abused—but not finished. Not yet.

The emotion of it made Charlie feel faint. He yelled with a tremble, heartbroken and exhausted, "I'm strong if you're strong. Are you strong?"

"I'm strong!" came the resounding reply.

Then it got blurry for Charlie and he sat. The boys hooted and held one another's arms aloft as Coach Picasso led them out the door and back onto the field.

CHAPTER .48

WHAT HAPPENED WOULD go down in the annals of Alabama high school football lore. Slowly, yard by yard, by big plays and dozens of smaller ones, by punch-counterpunch, guts, character, and sheer force of will, the Seminole Valley Bucks scratched their way back, but came up just short. It was a 23–21 slobber-knocker. They called it an instant classic and brilliantly played. A spectacle of timeless valor for both squads. A game that nobody should have to lose.

But lose they did.

Charlie was out of his mind proud and yet exhausted beyond comprehension. He had never felt so emotionally wrung out. The last hours of the evening had been the most crowded of his entire life. He was not prepared for it, and nearly collapsed time and time again. But those around him—Eve, fans, players, and coaches—would gather about him, hold him up, and entreat him to renew the fight.

Charlie just wanted to go into a hole and disappear. The

battle had taken its toll. The emotional roller coaster was now finished. After a few final words with the team and a few minutes spent at the subdued but well-deserved after party for the team, he just wanted to go home and be alone with his thoughts.

When the time seemed right he begged Eve to take him home, and they left.

PEPPERED THROUGHOUT OUR LIVES are moments that defy description. The ride home was one of those for Charlie. He fell into a beleaguered sleep. He may have dreamed. He woke to a dizzying, surreal sense of insanity beyond words. Every ounce of him felt spent and somehow abused. His heart was heavy beyond words. Max was gone. Beyond words. His team, though valiant in defeat, was beaten. He just needed to be alone to process it all.

When he got home he quickly retreated to his favorite easy chair in his dark study. He sank in deep, hoping that maybe in some way the pain would stop or that maybe miraculously he could disappear in the dark. It was nearly two in the morning. As he closed his eyes he heard that faint voice he'd heard over the months beckoning: *Lessons will be tested.* He wanted to scream at that voice to just please shut up. He'd been tested and failed, all right? He'd failed everything. He'd been beaten, stripped, and disfigured. He just wanted it all to stop. There were no words.

He opened his eyes long enough to spy the two un-opened letters he'd meant for Max lying in the half dark on the coffee table next to his chair. The two letters he'd kept out for Max that he never had a chance to share. Though in emotional tatters, he still recognized the moment. He'd been there when one of these letters was exactly the right potion at the right time.

Still slouching in the chair, he flicked on the table lamp and opened the first letter. It began, simply,

Was it worth it?

I had a friend of mine text me from Mobile this morning. His daughter got married last weekend and as she was leaving to go off on her honeymoon, from a distance he could read her lips. She was saying, "Where's my dad? Where's Daddy?" So he went over to her, and she handed him a note. And she hugged him and she left. And he opened up the note and the note said, "Daddy, I love you."

The rest of her note said, "If I was going to give you a Sunday school lesson I would ask you to answer this question. Was it worth it?"

That girl was smart. And the father said to me,

"Doc, from the maternity ward to the wedding chapel, it was worth it."

It was worth it.

I had to do a talk once, Charlie, and I was going to this place called KidsPeace, over in Lancaster, Pennsylvania. I had to fly in and rent a car. After I picked up the car, I drove to KidsPeace and they said, "Oh, we didn't know you were coming." I went to another building. They said, "I'm sorry, we didn't know you were coming. We are having an audit."

I finally got the guy who was supposed to bring me in. He said, "Oh, I forgot about it." It was a hellish day. This whole school, KidsPeace, is for kids that are challenged or troubled. They told them at the end of the day, as they were going home, that they should stay on campus because they weren't going home. "You are not going home, you are going to go listen to a motivational speaker." A couple of hundred kids.

That went over well.

I gave my talk and I talked about forgiveness. A girl came up to me when I was done and she said, "I didn't want to come to this. I was so mad when they told me to come. I'm at KidsPeace because I was shot by a drive-by shooter. He shot me in the chest. I don't know who he is. I was just standing on a corner and he shot me right in the chest. I've been so angry ever since." She said, "This is the first good day I've had since I've been shot. I am going to go forgive him. Everything I went through—it was worth it."

It was worth it.

I've got a little dog, Charlie. I'm crazy about this dog. Ella. A little Yorkie. I tell you I'm nuts about this dog. When I went to get it, a friend of mine, Patty, said, "Don't get that dog." I said, "Why not, Patty?" She said, "Because that dog will die and break your heart." And she's right. That dog will die. Did you know that love has a price? It's called grief. You never have to have a broken heart. How? Just don't love anything.

My dad went away to the South Pacific and fought during World War II. He saw a lot of awful things and then came home and drank his life away, to be honest with you. He sat on a barstool thinking about all the things that happened and grieving some of the things, I think. But I got him to a psychiatrist, an army psychiatrist, and he returned to church. The last fifteen or twenty years of his life were pretty good. And every once in a while I'll have a moment when I think, "Man, I wish my dad was here."

And every once in a while, I don't know if this makes sense, but I miss my dad real bad and yet I feel good missing him because I know that's the price I paid for loving him.

You had cancer. You moved people. You've become friends with children who have leukemia. You've inspired a city. Remember that. You've loved people and now they're gone. Was it worth it?

There's always a price. There's always a price. But see, Charlie, I like a life that has the highs. That means I'll take the lows. I hate the middle. You have to choose the life that you want.

Losing games, losing jobs, losing friends and loved ones. All these things are tough. Was it worth it? Because that's the price you pay for the things you go through. Was it worth it?

—The Sender

Charlie shifted in his chair, then attempted a cleansing sigh. Was it worth it, he wondered? He knew the answer would be yes when this grief had passed. He knew it. His pain subsided a bit as he lost himself in the story of the married girl, the little girl at KidsPeace that got shot, Ellabelle the Yorkie, the Sender's dad. The price of love is grief. Charlie felt like he could write a book about that. And he had a glimmer or reckoning that it was true.

He closed his eyes. Spent. Thinking about the worth of things. Wondering where God was in all this hurt. He dozed for a moment, then woke with a jerk. It felt like someone shook him and he sat up. He'd dropped the "Was it worth it?" letter and his hand rested on the last unread letter. His mind was suddenly sharp, wondering what had just happened, rubbing his fingers over the unopened envelope.

Feeling urgency, he opened the second letter. His mind became utterly sharp and clear. *Choose Didymus*, it read.

Charlie.

You're coming to the end of your chemo, but you are going through a couple of things here so I thought I'd pick up a few ideas and send you some love. I'm going to miss writing you these letters.

When I say the name Thomas, Thomas from the Bible, what comes to mind? You probably instantly think "doubting."

You know what's interesting? That's not in the Bible one time. He was never called "doubting Thomas." We labeled him. That's what we do. We look at other people and we put labels on them. We label children. We label other people. We should not label people. Not Thomas, not anyone.

The Bible calls Thomas Didymus. Didymus is Greek for "twin." What they are really saying about Thomas is he's a twin. There's a part of him that has doubt and fear. And there's a part of him that has faith and belief and love.

That's human nature, isn't it? To be of two minds about things. There are two Thomases and there's two mes and there's two Charlies.

We are all twins. The one that intimidates. The one that has self-interest in mind. And the one that wants to help other people beat a disease.

There's the one in us that wants to love strangers. Give to charity. And there's the one that wants to judge and gossip. Which twin emerges when you lose, Coach? Which twin emerges when somebody does something and it's really their own kind of pettiness? Which one emerges when you are tired?

Well, the twin that emerges is the one you feed. Whatever you feed grows. Whatever you starve dies. It's real easy. Whichever twin you feed grows. Feed the right twin.

If you feed yourself scripture and you pray for love

to come into your heart and you are actively kind to others, the twin that loves grows. If you hang around with a bunch of other people that are doing negative or illegal things and you affiliate with them, you start doing negative and illegal things.

Let me tell you the difference between choosing and feeling. I've tried to share so many things with you over the last few months. I've given you mantras, homework, stories, and advice. You have to choose to do them. You won't feel like doing them, you have to choose to do them. We've learned about winning on three levels, the spiritual, the physical, and the relational. You have to choose to do that. You may feel like being bitter, but you have to choose to be better. You may feel like living in the circumstance, but you have to choose to live in the vision. You may feel like giving up but you have to choose to fight weary. You may not feel like being kind but you have to choose to be a blessing. Same with forgiveness, being where your feet are, condition vs. position, fixin' to, I'm strong if you're strong. These are things you have to choose. You don't feel like puttin' down that Twinkie, you choose it, Dog.

We've laughed and learned, been tested and challenged. Hope it helped. Now get me that ring! And *remember that I love you and that you'll be tested and that you'll pass the tests. And remember that cancer doesn't care.*

And now we're done.

Wanna know the best speech I ever read? It was when Moses spoke to the Israelites before they went into the Promised Land. It was his very last speech. "Placed in front of you is life and death," he said. "Choose life." Bam! I don't know where you are right now, Charlie, but there's the whole story! Moses's final speech. Placed in front of Charlie Cristo is life and death. Choose. Placed in front of me is love and darkness every day. Choose love. Placed in front of you and me, Charlie, is faith and fear . . ."

Charlie put the letter down, closed his tired eyes, and sat in the depths of his chair, thinking about all that had happened. He was thinking about the lessons he'd learned and all the people he loved and if he'd ever have the opportunity or courage or faith to make any real difference again. Maybe he wasn't the right guy at the right time. Maybe he just wasn't. Maybe he was fooling himself.

Then again, maybe it was just a choice. The thought hit him like a roundhouse kick. His mind suddenly stopped spiraling as he grasped the most important lesson of all.

Choice. He opened his eyes and read the final line of the letter:

Choose faith, Didymus.

—The Sender

Acknowledgments

FROM BILL:

The book-writing process has a million moving parts. I'd like to say thanks to just a few of them. First, my writing partner, Kevin Elko: without your letters and persistent enthusiasm for a stricken coach, this book would not be. Thanks, too, to Pamela Clements and the entire team at Worthy Publishing for your matchless speed and hustle on this project. Thanks to Jamie Chavez, the ace of editors who has made us look *way* better at writing than we really are. Thanks as well to Lisa McBryde, RN, OCN—a true frontline warrior in the battle for the hearts, minds, and souls of cancer patients—for your real-life input on this manuscript. You've been a dedicated chemo nurse for twenty-five years, and your right words make all the difference. Thanks to Sharon Soldano of MD Anderson Cancer Center for your terrific heart and love for cancer fighters and for serving as a sounding board on the early ideas about this project. And, of course, to Denise: you are my friend, my muse, and the love of my life. Thank you for tolerating my drifting mind and never flinching when I was overcome with emotion at the bravery and courage I encountered in reading hundreds of cancer stories. You are such a big part of me, and thus such a big part of this story. Thank you.

And let me not forget the biggest piece of this whole story: the millions of people who suffer from cancer and yet fight through the pain and uncertainty with hope, courage, and vision. You may never know it, but you give us hope and reason to believe. God bless you all so much. Never quit. Never, never quit.

FROM KEVIN:

I would like to thank my friend Rob Burton for first discussing this project with me and helping me set in motion the process of creating it. I would like to thank Clyde Anderson for his belief in the project and all the wonderful people he put me in contact with. A thank-you goes to Sherry White for her friendship and directing us to the best publishing company we could have ever imagined. Thank you, Pamela Clements: you are without a doubt the most talented and caring person I have ever met in this business—you are exceptional.

To my friend and business partner, Shawn Kelly—they say you are only as strong as your team, and your innovation and consistency of personality makes us strong. To my incredible children, if God ever allowed me to choose I would definitely choose you two. A thank-you goes to my amazing wife, Karen, I grow every time we are together, and our daily talks of God's grace and our faith have forever changed me.

A thank-you to the best in the business, Coach Nick Saban. Our weekly talks have provided a lot of the material for this book. You have an exceptional mind and an even better heart. And finally to my best friend, Coach Chuck Pagano: that you chose me—or God chose us—to go your cancer journey together is something that will be stored away in my heart like a treasure until the grand day that God calls me home.

About the Authors

BILL BEAUSAY is a full-time author and professional speaker. He has written nearly a dozen books, including three national bestsellers on parenting, leadership, and communication, and is a popular speaker on business topics related to activating high-potential professionals. His A-list of clients includes Exxon-Mobil, GE, Transamerica, Cisco, MD Anderson, University of Michigan, MDRT/2016, and dozens of Fortune 500 companies. Find out more about Bill at www.billbeausay.com.

KEVIN ELKO is a performance consultant, motivational speaker, and author of four books. He received his bachelor's degree in biology education and coaching, then went on to West Virginia University, where he ultimately received his doctorate and was later inducted into West Virginia University Hall of Fame.

Elko's corporate clients have included ING, Tyson Foods, Abbott Labs, LPL Financial, The Hartford, Genworth, Jackson National Life, Pioneer Investments, Morgan Stanley, Bank of America, Merrill Lynch, and Sun

Life. He has worked with the Green Bay Packers and spoke to them the night before they defeated the Pittsburgh Steelers in the Super Bowl, the University of Alabama the night before they defeated LSU for the national championship, Alabama before they defeated Notre Dame for the national championship, and Florida State the night before they defeated Auburn for the national championship. Find out more about Kevin at www.drelko.com.

Bill Beausay

"The sincerity with which you delivered your content was absolutely unbelievable. It's not often a presenter, addressing a group of strangers for the first time, can make the connection you did with all of us. Heartfelt delivery, instant connection…a phenomenal presenter."

—Blake Johnson, President
Minard-Ames Insurance

You and I are living through one of the most amazing times in all recorded history. Opportunities of a lifetime await us on a daily basis in our businesses, our professions and our personal lives. Yet seeing those opportunities and seizing them is not always easy. It requires far ranging vision, courage, high performance leadership, grit, radiant confidence and a need to take action when the outcomes aren't always clear.

These are just some of the lessons of *The Sender*.

Bill has been working for decades building personal strength in people. He began writing and speaking in the early '90's and has become a popular Fortune 500 presenter, thought leader and motivator. Bill's goal has been steadfast: to create learning opportunities for groups and individuals to do more, make more and be more in their lives.

Whether you have a large or small group/team that needs motivation and focused persistence, or are in need of individual coaching to realize to your A-level potential, Bill is available to help.

Website: www.billbeausay.com
Email: bill@billbeausay.com

*To book either Dr. Elko or Bill Beausay
for a speaking engagement, please contact Shawn Kelly
at One Source Speakers, info@onesourcespeakers.com.*

IF YOU ENJOYED THIS BOOK, WILL YOU CONSIDER SHARING THE MESSAGE WITH OTHERS?

Mention the book in a blog post or through Facebook, Twitter, Pinterest, or upload a picture through Instagram.

Recommend this book to those in your small group, book club, workplace, and classes.

Head over to facebook.com/worthypublishing, "LIKE" the page, and post a comment as to what you enjoyed the most.

Tweet "I recommend reading #TheSender by @billbeausay // @drkevinelko //@worthypub"

Pick up a copy for someone you know who would be challenged and encouraged by this message.

Write a book review online.

Visit us at worthypublishing.com

twitter.com/worthypub

worthypub.tumblr.com

facebook.com/worthypublishing

pinterest.com/worthypub

instagram.com/worthypub

youtube.com/worthypublishing